The Dead Past

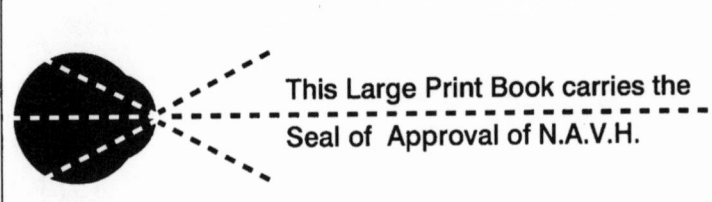

This Large Print Book carries the
Seal of Approval of N.A.V.H.

The Dead Past

LT
M
14

TOM PICCIRILLI

Thorndike Press • Thorndike, Maine

Published in 1999 by arrangement with DHS Literary, Inc.

Thorndike Large Print ® Senior Lifestyles Series.

The tree indicium is a trademark of Thorndike Press.

The text of this Large Print edition is unabridged.
Other aspects of the book may vary from the original edition.

Set in 16 pt. Plantin by Minnie B. Raven.

Printed in the United States on permanent paper.

Library of Congress Cataloging-in-Publication Data

Piccirilli, Tom.
    The dead past : a mystery / by Tom Piccirilli.
        p.   cm.
    ISBN 0-7862-1833-9 (lg. print : hc : alk. paper)
    1. Large type books.   I. Title.
    [PS3566.I266D42   1999]
    813'.54—dc21   98-56659

Let the dead Past bury its dead.
— Longfellow, *A Psalm of Life*

*For Ed Gorman and Buddy Howe,
both of whom know the past is
only taking a siesta.*

1

When my eyes focused, I saw that the clock read 4:10.

A phone call at four in the morning can only mean one of two things: either my ex-wife is on a crying jag about her latest biker boyfriend, or else my grandmother is caught up in something which will probably get me killed.

With great conviction I promised God a fifty per cent tithe of my annual net if only I'd hear Michelle's usual complaints about the harsher realities of living with men who wear leather underwear and have BORN TO KILL WIMPS tattooed across their chests.

But the familiar sense of trepidation was already wedged into the pit of my stomach. I cleared my throat, reached over and snatched the receiver before it rang again. "Hello?"

"Jonathan," my grandmother said. "I realize it's quite late and I hate to disturb you at this hour, but there's been trouble here in Felicity Grove."

I did some quick math and figured I should've offered God my gross worth and two certificates of deposit instead. "Anna, there's trouble everywhere if you go looking for it."

"I do not," she emphasized, "go looking for it."

That might be the truth, I thought, knowing how she kept to herself and her books most of the time. Still, I wondered how anybody not affiliated with the bomb squad, Mafia, or the CIA could get involved with so much calamity. Especially in a town where the population is less than ten thousand. "Well, whatever. Let the police take care of it. Haven't you learned not to rush into murder cases that have nothing to do with you? After the last time?"

There was a long pause while she turned that one over. "I didn't say anything about murder."

"No, but you wouldn't have phoned me at four in the morning otherwise."

She sighed, and I could hear the soft squeak of tires as she wheeled herself around the kitchen, running the tap and putting tea on. "You need to return home immediately," she stated flatly. "It was presumptuous of me but I've already taken the liberty of calling the airport. The first flight back leaves Kennedy at seven fifty-five this morning. I'll have a cab meet you."

It always sounded so easy to put my entire life on hold when she ordered it in that voice. "I can't close up the store on a moment's notice just because you've gotten your nose stuck in somebody else's business again."

"This is not . . ."

"Last week I bought several rare volumes of *Nicht Wahr?* from two German antiquarian collectors. The books are expected tomorrow and I have to be on hand to sign for them."

"Couldn't one of your employees simply forge your name?" she said. "What possible difference would it make to the German sellers?"

None, but I was still half asleep and it was the best excuse I could come up with to keep from doing what I knew I was going to do anyway.

There are times you must go home to a place that is no longer home — and if that's not swinging in full circle, then at least it's moving backwards. Wolfe was wrong: you can never *get away* from home. I stood and brushed the curtains aside from the window, staring at the snow on Amsterdam Avenue glowing with the last strands of moonlight; in an hour it would be a convulsive churning of grime. In New York, February is a month bearing no resemblance to the winters of my childhood. "There's another foot of snow on the ground. That means the drifts are at least four feet high in Felicity Grove."

"Approximately," she said with some bite now. She mistook my moment of sentiment for more arguing on my part. Unlike most of the emotions she kept a tight rein on, disappointment often bled through.

"Please don't try to make me feel guilty because I don't want to come rushing back on a whim, Anna."

The tea pot whistled, and her rotweiller, Anubis, made slow, stalking sounds across the kitchen tiles. He sounded nervous, and that bothered me. "I wouldn't dream of calling you on simple caprice, Jonathan. I need your help, and not merely for legwork. Besides, nobody can make you feel guilty except yourself."

"That's a self-serving cliché I don't accept. Of course you can do it to me."

My grandmother has a smile that can be heard from across a room. "Really? I hadn't noticed."

"Okay," I said, fully awake. My curiosity was peaked, and if there's one nasty character trait I've inherited from her it's that I'm nosy, too. "Maybe I can take a few days off. Give me an overview, Anna. What's it all about?"

She took a breath and called Anubis to her. "Evidence has been introduced into the death of Margaret Gallagher. The police now believe it may have been a homicide."

Margaret had owned a flower stand at the corner of Monroe and Fairlawn in Felicity Grove for as long as I could remember. I had known her to be a woman with a boisterous laugh, and she had let me skimp a couple bucks on my prom date's corsage. She'd died a few months ago of natural causes. "What evidence? You told me she had a heart attack."

"And so she did, but three days ago a young man named Richie Harraday tried to dispense with several pieces of jewelry at a local pawn shop. Unfortunately for him, the owner of the shop had originally sold the pieces to Margaret some months earlier — a silver oval locket, and a smaller, distinctive clover-shaped one. He remembered them quite well because she'd asked him to engrave each with a specific flower pattern. The sheriff was called in, and a subsequent check of her belongings showed the jewelry to be missing. The police suspect that Richie Harraday burglarized Margaret's home, and during the robbery she was either attacked or frightened badly enough to have suffered cardiac arrest. If such is the case, then under the Felony Murder Doctrine Harraday is responsible for her death and the charge will be murder."

"What does Harraday say?"

"He told the pawnbroker he discovered the lockets in the park, but when the police performed a more thorough search of Margaret's home, they found that the back screen window had been partially cut through. Harrady's prints were all over the inside pane of glass."

"Even so, how could the cops possibly prove he had anything to do with her death?"

"I doubt they could have."

Something in her tone hooked me. "Could have?"

"Yes. Richie Harraday fled before he could be arrested. He was already known to the police as a juvenile delinquent. Petty crimes for the most part. Disturbing the peace, car theft and the like."

"I don't get it, Anna. Exactly what do you expect me to do? Hunt this guy down?"

"No, Jonathan," she said, sipping more tea, "that won't be necessary." The dog was whining, something I'd never heard him do before. "Richie Harraday's body was found in my garbage can nearly four hours ago."

2

When I got out of luggage claims I saw Lowell Tully sitting in the airport coffee shop, reading the *Felicity Grove Gazette* and eating a stack of waffles reinforced by a bulwark of sausages. His muscles rippled beneath his brown Deputy's uniform like tectonic plates shifting, the veins in his corded neck bulging. I suddenly wished I'd taken more of an interest in those Soloflex commercials.

It didn't seem as though he waited for anyone in particular, laid back and enjoying his meal, but I knew he was there for me. He didn't read the paper unless he was killing time: the front page of the gazette read MERLIN'S TURKEY TAKES COUNTY PRIZE. Nobody read the paper unless they were killing time. I stepped over and put my suitcase down, sat beside him and waved the waitress over.

"You know what I said to myself not more than twenty minutes ago?" he asked.

"What was that?"

"I said, 'It's been a long while since I've seen Johnny Kendrick, I wonder how he's

13

doing?' And then I stop in here for breakfast and up you come walking right under my nose."

He still looked the same as when we'd played varsity football together almost ten years ago. Most of his face was eclipsed by a large, boyish smile that used to turn cheerleaders into lemmings that would follow him off any cliff. He had slightly suspicious eyes too bright to be considered beady, yet he occasionally dropped into an Eastwood squint that would set any wisemouth back a few paces. His first year on the force, I'd seen him break up a pool room brawl by dislocating every third guy's arm. He earned his respect the old-fashioned way. If Lowell and I weren't exactly best friends, I was certainly glad we weren't enemies.

"It happens like that sometimes," I said.

He re-doubled his attack on his breakfast and was finished before the waitress came with my coffee. "Come on," he said. "I'll drive you into town."

We walked to his squad car parked directly out front, and I noticed the cab that Anna had sent for me. I paid the driver for his time and let him go, then got in beside Lowell, overly aware of the shotgun locked vertically between the seats. "Is this standard issue now?"

"The Grove's changed some." He frowned. "You'll never believe it, but I've started repeating things my father used to tell me. I'm not sure how I feel about that."

"For example?"

"Well, get this, I caught myself the other day saying 'when I was a boy we always slept with our windows open.'" He grimaced, and it surprised me at just how much of his father I did see in him at that moment. "In exactly the same disgusted tone my old man always used."

I frowned too because, like him, I couldn't remember if we'd actually done that or if it was just something our parents had told us too often. "I think I know what you mean."

"I've also been quoting prices a lot whenever I go shopping. It all makes me sound cheap and bitter, and I'm neither."

"If there's one person I don't consider a cynic, Lowell, it's you."

We crept down the highway through the snowy lanes; traffic was negligible, but even taking the weather into account he drove especially slow. It was as if he was giving a stranger a grand tour of the township, a proud papa showing off his baby. Canadian winds blew off Lake Ontario across northern New York, freezing everything; when he turned off the highway we entered a new world carved out by the blizzard. Canopy trees cocooned in frost, utility wires and poles heavy with rime, and six-foot-high waves of white unfurled across the drainage ditches as we continued down into Felicity Grove. Cars were cluttered into driveways, making room for the plows. The evergreens and pines added an emerald hue to the frost on the windshields.

There was silence in the car except for the occasional crackle of static and indecipherable murmurs over the police radio. Since the official investigation into Richie Harraday's murder was still under way, anything Lowell told me would be off the record. If Merlin's turkey could make the headline then word of murder was going to have them cleaning their rifles. Rather than push for information, I let Lowell broach the subject first. It wasn't a long wait.

"This one confuses the hell out of me," he said. "And the more I mull it over the more scattered the implications become."

"How so?"

"I can't see why anyone would want to kill Richie Harraday. He was strictly a nickel and dime operator. He had no money or drugs to steal."

Living in the city had taught me many things, and one of them was that nobody

16

needed a reason to kill you. Out here it was still different, I hoped. "Maybe it was something personal. Was he chasing the wrong guy's wife?"

Lowell's lips flattened, and his shoulders rose like hilltops as he shrugged. "Not that we know of. I kept a pretty close eye on him since his last arrest, and he seemed to have kept to the narrow. Frankly, I never thought he'd have the guts to burgle a house." His squint returned. "And then he goes and gets himself killed off a couple days later. Over what? Where's the connection?" He grunted, harsh and low, the way Anubis did. "And the possibility exists that there is no connection. That we're just dealing with some sicko and a random killing."

"Do you believe that?"

"No, but it's something I've got to think about."

My next question was the rough one. "Do you think Anna was deliberately involved?"

"I don't know about that either, and I'd hate to hazard a guess. It doesn't make much sense one way or the other."

I agreed with him. My grandmother's house did not lie at the end of Little Red Riding Hood's path through the woods, but it was a corner home set almost directly across the back woods of a park, where the brush overgrew into thickets. Neighbors on either side were more than fifty yards away down the ends of the block. I'd never thought about how secluded a place it actually was. Conceivably, Harraday's corpse was simply dumped there because it was a conveniently remote area. But why leave him in the trash can where he was sure to be found? Why not hide the body in the woods where it might not be discovered for days, maybe weeks?

I didn't want to think that somebody had chosen Anna for a particular reason.

"How did he die?" I asked.

Lowell checked his watch. "Haven't gotten the coroner's report yet, but Wallace should be done in a little while, around noon. Harraday's neck was broken though, that much is certain, but it might have occurred when the killer or killers were jamming him head first into your granny's pail."

"What a lovely thought. No other signs of struggle? Footprints in the snow?"

"The way it was coming down last night anything would have been covered in a matter of minutes."

Icicles gleamed from low hanging branches and dropped onto the hood of the car as we passed. "Where was he for the past three days between the time he brought the jewelry to the pawnshop until they found his body?"

"Nobody's saying for certain, but he was probably right at home. We watched the house as best we could, but he lived out in a trailer by the edge of town, and there are plenty of logging paths back there."

"He live alone?"

"No, with his brother Maurice."

"Get out of here," I said.

Lowell chuckled. "I heard his mother named him after Chevalier, which probably explains why he's got such a nasty disposition. Everybody calls him Tons. He's about thirty-five, a troublemaker but not clever enough to be a real problem. Sold a little cocaine and stole some farm equipment for a few years, but then he got married last spring and had a baby girl. That seemed to get him turned around and settled down. You can never be completely sure, though."

"Did he ever change his name?"

"No."

We crossed in front of the county courts where a large gazebo and cast-iron fountain embellish the town square. "You know why I picked you up, don't you?" he asked. "And why I'm not going to go into my usual lecture about how you should hold your granny back and let the cops handle the investigation?"

19

"Yes." He was nervous, too. "Was there a note?"

"If there was, it wouldn't be made public knowledge."

I needed to ascertain if a note had been left behind for my grandmother, and now I knew there hadn't been or else Lowell would've found a way to tell me. We pulled up in front of Anna's house, and I got my first look at the place where Richie Harraday's body had been disposed of. The snow was trampled by the police and a hole with a ten foot circumference had been dug in the search for physical evidence.

"Anything at all?"

"No. Tell Anna I'll be stopping in on her from time to time. If you need me, just holler."

"You really say that, don't you, Lowell? You say, 'holler' not 'give me a call.' You say holler."

"I say holler. So did my father. So did you."

"I don't think so. Thanks for the lift."

My grandmother's house wasn't at the end of a path through the woods, but there was still a bad wolf or two around. Lowell and I might not have slept with our windows open as children, and those homespun tales our fathers told us about childhoods free

from fear could have been merely gingerbread spicing. Maybe there had never been
any real safety in Felicity Grove.

I was glad he had the shotgun. If I had to,
I'd holler like a banshee owl.

3

I walked up the shoveled path and the front door opened, storm window swinging back against the wood railing with a crash as Anna wheeled herself onto the porch to greet me. Anubis never strayed from her side, gazing over the yard like he was lord of the manor.

Once again I was taken by how much they occasionally acted as parts of the same being, the rotweiller's muscle and ferocity tied in an odd fashion to my grandmother's cool depth of intelligence and character. Six years together had taught them to move as one, the dog's paws never getting caught beneath the tires of her wheelchair, and Anna rarely having to move her hand more than a few inches to pat Anubis' head. Even the similarity of their names seemed a symbiosis of some kind.

At sixty-eight, Anna Kendrick was as lovely as any woman twenty years her junior. She had that handsome, womanly quality that lasts long after nubile waifs have lost their giggly, lip-nibbling charm. In the three decades since her husband had died, my grandmother had been offered more marriage proposals than the entire ladies auxiliary rotary club.

As an adolescent, her hair had been the sharply yellow color of whey, and then in her teenage years it had changed to a premature, full and beautiful silver. Since that time, it had never turned white or gray. My grandmother showed few signs of age; her face was nearly free of wrinkles, except for the deepened crow's feet tracks about her eyes and those thicker parentheses around the mouth. Her lips were the true definition of pert, though if I ever said that out loud she'd probably deck me. Despite the wheelchair, there was nothing feeble about her. Strength radiated. Her vision remained twenty-twenty, and biceps bulged beneath her wool sweaters. People mistakenly assumed she'd crocheted the sweaters, but knitting had actually been my mother's love. Anna had been bestowed boxes of cardigans and pullovers.

"Jonathan," she said. "You're looking well. Thank you for coming on such short notice."

She made it sound like we were meeting for a sales committee. I was dumbstruck for a moment, the conversation with Lowell weighing in my thoughts. "Are you all right, Anna?"

"Of course, dear, why do you ask?"

Anubis trotted down the ramp beside the porch stairs and gave my hand a couple of swipes of his broad tongue — that action alone made him about four hundred times more friendly to me than he would ever be with anybody else besides my grandmother — before he turned and stalked away.

"You must be famished," Anna said. "I've been preparing much of the morning. Let's have a late breakfast." She glanced at the icy ground. "Please be careful of the ramp. The boys who shoveled didn't put down as much salt as they should have."

Once inside she kissed my cheek, and I took her hand and pushed the chair to the head of the dining room table. Settings and dishes had been laid out, and I could see she'd spent all morning on one of her usual extravagant feasts. She liked to cook and always went overboard. More food was in view than four people could eat, unless maybe Lowell was invited for brunch. I dropped my bags, took off my coat and draped it on the old-fashioned rack in the corner.

There are times you must return home to a place that is no longer home, and you might startle yourself with how easily the movements become familiar again. How quickly you fall back into the same routines, and how at ease you feel coming back to them.

I stepped into the kitchen and brought out what she'd made, dish by dish though we'd never eat it all. I tried not to ruminate while she fixed me a heaping plate: Eggs Benedict, French toast, buttered bagels, hash browns, and enough bacon to harden my arteries just by staring at it. She always cooked as if we had a large family left.

"I can only assume that Deputy Tully picked you up at the airport for a specific reason?"

"Not really," I said.

She smiled. "He knew I'd call you immediately, and realized you'd take the first flight in. He's a bright and caring man, even if a bit stand-offish. He deserves to be in charge of our police force more so than Sheriff Broghin." Her lips curled when she said his name, and I wondered for the nth time if it was true that they'd been lovers five decades ago. I'd never gotten up the guts to ask her though I knew she'd tell me the truth. I didn't want to think about how narrowly I'd avoided being related to Broghin. "I'm obligated to ask . . . have they discovered anything new since last night?"

This was going to be some meal, all right.

"Lowell didn't say much."

"Eat, dear, eat."

I tried to eat, answer, and not talk with my mouth full all at the same time and nearly choked to death.

"Swallow, dear, swallow."

"He told me that Wallace's report would be ready" — I glanced at the kitchen clock — "right about now."

"Good. We'll phone when we've finished eating."

"Don't get pushy, Anna. It took us a while to mend a few neighborly fences after your last couple of encounters with Broghin and Wallace."

"I would not call them, in effect, *my* encounters. If two men in such a professional capacity as they are inclined to let ego and petty rivalries get in the way of serving the common good, then it only proves my point that we must, on occasion, circumvent these by-the-book police investigations."

I glanced over at her bookstand and saw that she'd been reading too much goddamn Miss Marple again.

"Easy for you to say, Anna; it wasn't you who spent time in a cell with a drunk who cried all night long about spiders crawling out of his eyes."

"I can't argue that."

"At last."

"But are you willing to allow that the police *can* overlook the more . . . imaginative crimes, due to their formal training?"

"I'd rather have spiders crawl out of my eyes than answer that." How could I deny it, considering she and I had helped Broghin out six times in as many years, tracking down two blackmailers, a child-napper, and three murderers, including the filth who had killed my parents?

But my grandmother hadn't spent time in a county jail cell for contempt of court or resisting arrest, and I had. And while a cell in Felicity Grove was vastly different than one on Rikers Island, it was still no picnic waking up for nearly three months with bars surrounding you.

She also hadn't been slashed across the chest with a Bowie knife, shot a half inch above her kidneys, or had her left clavicle broken twice. And as rotten as jail was, a hospital bed was even uglier, with tubes jammed in your nostrils and mouth and sticking out of your forearms, blood and sugar dripping the entire sleepless night like the Chinese water torture, with catheters shoved up my personally favorite organ, one which should definitely not have things shoved up it.

"This is different," I told her. This had a personal touch to it, with a corpse left right out front like a calling card or a private message, or worse, a dare. That frightened the hell out of me.

"Perhaps."

"It's called obstructing justice, Anna."

"It's justice, period," she said with finality. Anubis noticed the edge in her voice and lifted his head beside her. We were and weren't arguing about the same thing; I wanted answers too, and I had no compunction with going around Broghin or anybody else if I felt it was necessary. Six years ago it had been, and I'd sidestepped the overweight, tobacco-chewing, walking-short sheriff and the rest of his department, and I'd do it again if I had to.

I ate without much appetite. Talking about murder over eggs just wasn't an appealing combination so far as I was concerned. Distracted, I felt my attention continually being tugged away from what I was saying. Something about the house was different, I thought, but I couldn't be sure, and the harder I glanced about the room the stronger the feeling became.

"What is it?" she asked.

The photographs on the living room wall had been changed: frames held new pictures. My parents smiled out from behind clinked champagne glasses; me as a kid on a tricycle had been replaced by me as a kid scribbling with crayons; plenty of people I didn't know grinned and laughed and shmoozed for the camera: four young women in uncomfortable-looking swimwear sat by a pool laughing, and my grandfather sat posing in a recliner with a copy of Steinbeck's *The Wayward Bus* opened on his lap.

"You've noticed," Anna said.

"I know that I'm getting way too maudlin, but you too?"

"Sentimental perhaps, but that's not entirely the reason why. Last week I was cleaning out that junk closet and found a great many old letters. Thoughts of one friend turned to another and another, like dominoes of memory, and soon I was digging in other closets as well, looking through photo albums that haven't been opened for years."

"I like the change."

"At first, I wasn't sure if I would, having grown so accustomed to the way things were. But I enjoy the shift in the scenery, if you will."

I went to the wall and studied the age-cracked photographs. There was a picture of my mother, taken when she was maybe ten, sitting on the curb just outside with a skirtful of tulips, playing with a black kitten while a sprinkler shot a high arc of water behind them. Seeing the front of the house from that angle dredged up a question I'd been meaning to ask. "Who discovered the body here at midnight, Anna? This morning you said, 'His body was found in my garbage can . . .'"

The smile stayed stapled to her face but the warmth fled. "I should have clarified the point. Jim Witherton was returning home from his night security job. In the blizzard he noticed something odd on the lawn as he drove by but couldn't be certain as to what. Apparently it stuck with him and a few minutes later he walked back down the block and discovered Richie Harraday in his unenviable position. Jim woke me then and I telephoned the police immediately."

"He stayed with you?"

"Yes, until the sheriff and Deputy Tully arrived. He's now employed with Syntex computer labs over in Norwood County. Are you familiar with it?"

"Yes." They had their own private security force at Syntex, and I'd heard that the training program was as difficult as the police academy; good, that made me feel a little better, knowing that a rent-a-cop was only up the block. "How long did it take for

Broghin to arrive?"

She paused and considered. "No more than ten or fifteen minutes."

"Did you inspect the area before he got here?"

"No," was the flat answer she gave — chin held high, gathering a haughty air about her like a sweater — but she said a lot more with her eyes. I know my grandmother in ways that parents can never know their children, to a point that most siblings will never arrive. I remembered how Anubis had whined, picking up the vibes of his mistress. I knew she had been terrified last night. Did she see more than she was telling? Was Anna hiding something?

"Will you call Wallace or shall I?" she asked.

"You can do it."

"Fine. Afterwards, I think we will begin with —"

"No," I said. "Before anything else, I want to visit the cemetery."

This house was full of ghosts, those of my parents and those of our making. Blood followed blood. The dead could stuff your lungs if you let them. "I should go, too. I haven't been quite as conscientious in the past weeks as I should have been, but the weather often makes it difficult for me."

"I wasn't chastising you, Anna."

I wondered if Richie Harraday's brother, Maurice, would visit him a lot. Anna kept an eye on the photographs, on herself and the unsaved. "I would accompany you but I realize you'd rather go alone."

"That's true," I said, "but right now I'm going to buy some flowers."

Gouts of snow and slush spattered the windshield. I drove Anna's van downtown; learning to use the hand controls had been hellish in the beginning, and I was thankful I remained adept.

Even with the cold I kept the window down. The air felt good in my face — I must've looked like Anubis when he came for a ride, his snout turned into the breeze — with room to move and air to breathe and no steel monoliths or crackheads hogging the view. In a couple of days I'd be bored out of my socks with the town, but for the moment I enjoyed the change in atmosphere.

I'd been wondering what had happened to Margaret Gallagher's flower shop after her death, whether it had been closed or put under new management. I would miss Margaret's chattiness and empathy, and all the flowers and kind words she'd given me since the death of my parents.

I made a left onto Fairlawn and passed the shop. There was a WE'RE OPEN sign on the door, so I parked at the curb and walked in. Chimes that had never been there before tinkled as I entered.

On rare occasions life unfolds like a series of scenes from a good movie.

You step into, say, a flower shop, and there is a girl with her back towards you. It is an extremely sexy back, and you don't even try to make an effort to understand how a back can be sexy. You take what you can get. She turns slowly in your direction, this owner of the back, and you see, inch by inch as she completes her turn, that the front is as beautiful as the back. Her face is a compendium of all the lovely features you want to be there; the dark hair falls in thick curls that frame her face in such a way as to highlight each quality; animate green eyes like a fortune in jade, a smile both luscious and yet unintimidating. Most people would say the freckles across her nose had been "splashed" there, but you disagree. Each seems painstakingly placed to perfectly underscore those eyes, smooth skin, the dimples and sleek jawline, and you learn something of her life by each soft etching of furrow in her forehead.

You hope she is not as crazy as your ex-wife.

Of course, by this point she is asking, "Can I help you?" for the third time and you are staring like an idiot.

I snapped out of it and smiled, trying my best not to fawn too blatantly, and failing. "Uhm, ah, I'd like to buy some flowers," was my stimulating response. I could feel my IQ plummet to below sea level.

She proved to be kind, though, and didn't make an issue out of my obvious stupidity. "Well, you've come to the right place then." She laughed gently and Cupid nailed me in the chest with another batch of arrows. I promised God not to be so chintzy this time if only this girl would marry me before sunset.

She had one of those crooked grins that clamp down at the ends, adding a round friendliness to her face. It was then I noticed she looked familiar. "Were you looking for anything in particular, or just a bouquet?"

"Tulips," I answered.

She led me to the refrigerated area in the back where the fresh flowers were stored. She went through the racks, shoving various bins aside, opening other doors and pulling out different types of flora, but no tulips. "I'm sorry, but we're out. I'm new at this and having a heck of a time getting the proper ordering forms in to the right people."

It was the break I needed to ask her her name. "I was sorry to hear about Margaret," I said. It sounded flat and insincere because it was the kind of statement that can't be prettied up. I tried thinking of something else to say but it all sounded equally lackluster.

"Thank you," she said warmly, with a note of appreciation.

I knew Margaret had never had any children, but I played the hand out. "Were you her . . . ?"

"Niece. Her great-niece actually, her sister's granddaughter, but I always called her my aunt. Anything else would have sounded distant, and we weren't. It's been a while since I've visited Felicity Grove, but we always kept in touch. My family's originally from San Diego." She seemed very much the child in that moment, and a needle jabbed at a memory at the bottom of my mental junk drawer.

"Wait a second," I said. A tenuous, hazy image came into slightly more focus. "Is your name . . . Kathy?"

"Katie, yes."

"Did you used to play with . . . uhm, like a

little oven thingie that baked real cup-
cakes?"

"How do you know that!" she exclaimed,
jade eyes beaming as brightly as her smile.

"I ate two or three of them."

Anna used to stop by to chat with Margaret on summer days when I was a boy. On
a few visits Margaret had a shy girl sitting in
the front of the store with an orchid in her
hair, playing with tea sets and Barbie mobile
homes and ersatz ovens. That's really all the
recollections I could get a hold on, except
for the fact that I had eaten a couple of the
inedible cakes.

Katie grabbed my forearm and laughed.
"That's right, I used to like visiting Aunt
Margaret because there were so many kids
to play with." She stared intently at me and
motioned with her fingers as if she were
slicing years off my face. "I think I remember you now."

She didn't, but it was a nice thing to say.
"They tasted like styrofoam."

"Ugh, the worst, but I must've made a
hundred of them."

"How many did you eat?"

"None, of course. What, you think I've
got a death wish?"

I enjoyed her mannerisms; personality
shined through in her body language, and I

liked the way it talked. She leaned back and crossed her arms, giving me the once over, then ran her forefinger along her bottom lip, which brought my attention even more fully to her mouth.

"I don't know your name," she said.

"Jonathan Kendrick."

"Pleased to meet you *again*, Jonathan."

"It's been . . ."

I spotted him through the window.

He was waving his arms wildly at me and skip-walking across the street, his raggedy overcoat flopping out behind him in the breeze. A truck horn blared and epithets were shouted, but he just happily waved to the driver.

I wasn't sure if Katie had ever met him before, but if she hadn't, I knew what she was going to think when he bounded in. Most people were immediately frightened, and you couldn't blame them.

I said, "Cripes," but didn't have time to tell Katie anything before the door burst open in a flurry of black motion, the bells jangling madly.

"Hello . . . ?" she asked, wheeling.

"I am Crummler!" he shouted, rushing her like he was blitzing a quarterback. "I am here!"

Katie virtually leaped into my chest with a

muffled shriek, arms tightly hugging around my neck. I enjoyed this mannerism of hers even more than the others, though the choke-hold could easily crush my windpipe. She winced and looked over her shoulder at him, staring at the wild man standing three feet away.

"We've talked about personal space before, Crummler," I said.

Zebediah Crummler could have been the poster boy for the word "wiry." His body and his hair were wiry, and his mind was like a red-hot copper wire with too much juice going through it. He was always in motion, and I couldn't imagine him in any state of repose. Impossible to imagine him not wound up tighter than a clock about to blow a few coils. He bounced and shivered and shuddered; yet for all that, most of the running current was internal, and you could see how it flowed through his veins. No one who knew him was afraid of him, but he made strangers leap onto kitchen counters or into the chests of the hopelessly romantic. Being in such proximity of sheer exuberance, when there is nothing visible to be exuberant about, can be a terrifying situation.

"I have returned!" Crummler yelled.

"From where?" I asked.

"Know you not, Jon?" he said, peering at me.

"I know not."

"Then I shall tell you."

"Oh lord," Katie whispered in my ear.

"I have been in battle," Crummler went on, his voice hushed. "With *forces*."

"I see."

"Jeez, what forces?" Katie asked.

"Know you not?"

"I know not," she said.

"This could get repetitious," I said.

"They fear me for I am Crummler! These forces of an ancient and dark domain." His eyebrows danced like horny caterpillars. "Who reign in far off dimensions where obsidian towers rise through the ochre night and desert winds blow the sand of ages across the ruins of a thousand lost civilizations and the world . . ."

I cut him off. "Do you want a ride back to the cemetery, Crummler? I'm heading that way."

"The cemetery?" Katie murmured out the side of her mouth.

"I would like for you to give me a ride back to the cemetery, Jon. My feet hurt. I have a hole in my shoe and the snow makes my toes cold."

"Okay," I nodded. "You know Anna's van

right over there. The door on the passenger side is open. Wait for me and I'll be out in a minute."

He told me okay and went off much more calmly than he'd come in, glad that he had someone who'd listen to him. As if just now realizing she had her arms around me, Katie glanced down from my neck, let go and stepped away.

"In case you didn't catch it," I said, "that was Crummler."

"I caught it, and he's going to catch a swift kick if he ever comes in here like that again. You mind telling me if I have that to look forward to every afternoon?"

There was a dropped hint in that statement that said she was planning on remaining in Felicity Grove indefinitely.

"I take it you've never seen him before."

"No, wouldn't I remember? I must've missed him because he's been in that dark domain for so long."

I chuckled and she did too, letting out a lot of nervous laughter, and then we stood facing each other for a few seconds before Crummler began beeping the van horn. "It was nice meeting you," I told her.

"I'm sorry we didn't have tulips. But I promise I'll track down those orders for you. Why don't you come back in a couple of days and see if they're here?"

Yeah, why not?

I drove Crummler to a shoe store and bought him a pair of work boots before I took him back to the cemetery. Someone without much wit had dubbed the place *Felicity Grave,* and to the town's shame, the name stuck. I listened to Crummler's excited prattling the way an adult is forced to listen to a child's jabbering about cartoons or comic books or squirrels chasing nuts in the back yard. Every once in a while I let out an "ooh" and an "ah." He rallied back and forth with himself, shifting gears between highly detailed stories of knights and demon dragons to what he had for breakfast — franks and beans — to a ghost that walked the edge of the graveyard and scared him by flinging willow branches at his shack, to how warm his feet were, to an assortment of other weird mental meanderings.

I liked Crummler because he kept the cemetery more well-kept than a gardener keeps his azaleas. It was not hyperbole to say that his job was his life; Zebediah Crummler had been a ward of the state for decades, and his lost existence before he came to Felicity Grove was nothing but the confines of orphanages, foster homes, and mental hospitals around New York State. Like a snapping electrical line, his manic persona needed grounding, and being caretaker of the graveyard gave his life meaning. You could hear the excitement in his voice when he talked of visitors who'd commented on the landscaping, the pure joy of being indispensable. Crummler meant something to himself as much as he did to the town, and I didn't think I could say that about more than a handful of other people I knew.

He got out of the van and walked with me to the graves of my parents. He said, "Say hello to your folks for me, Jon." I promised him I would and watched him race across the snow drifts back to his home.

I kneeled in the snow, touching the tombstones out of some sense of respect. Sometimes I thought Crummler must actually clean each grave separately, a feather duster in one hand and a polishing rag in the other. The trees were trimmed, evergreens pruned, the leaves always raked so that the cemetery looked more like a park than a place for the dead. The snow and ice added new sculptures to this museum, and I wasn't sure whether I should be embarrassed by the pleasure I felt in simply spending a little time here.

The frozen earth crackled and rustled beneath my feet as I walked back to the van. Crummler waved from his shack near the surrounding stone wall, fenced-in by spiked gates like those at Dracula's castle. It only added to the eccentricity of the place, as though we should all know that graveyards are only a kind of playground where you ate franks and beans and ran into ghosts with willow swatches. Crummler kept waving and waving, both arms in the air as if he was guiding planes to safe landings. He laughed and called out more of his Crummler talk, frantic and hysterical and filled with meanings I would never understand.

I hoped.

4

It began snowing again as I drove back to Anna's. The wind rose to beat and twine the wafting flakes into spiraling sheets around the van. An odd mood descended, partly darkened by recalling murder yet buoyed by meeting Katie, and this time I got to do it without the styrofoam cakes.

I got out of the van feeling like one of those skaters in a glass globe, the world shaken up stuck behind transparent walls. Stasis, for the moment, but something would give soon. The spot where Richie Harraday had died on the lawn had already been covered with fresh snow. I clopped slush off my shoes, and walked into the foyer. Anubis snapped forward growling until he recognized me, then settled back on his haunches at Anna's side, mildly perturbed. My grandmother put Agatha Christie's final novel *Sleeping Murder* on her reading stand and grimaced sadly at me.

"Uh oh," I said.

Her lips were thin, like my father's had been, and smoothed out thinner still. "You were right, Jonathan. It doesn't pay to be too pushy with our local constabulary."

"And just what does that mean?"

"I may have already committed the first faux pas of this case."

I couldn't stand it when she called our — *experiences* or whatever the hell they were — cases. They weren't cases. A case was what you put suits in, or books. It was twenty-four beers packed into cardboard. It's what lawyers take to make money, and what prosecutors fail at too often. But for those exceptions, I didn't want to think that cases have anything to do with me.

"What happened, Anna?"

"I held off from immediately phoning the morgue. Instead, I spent the afternoon reading until a few minutes ago when I called Wallace and inquired into what progress had been made in determining Harraday's death."

"And?"

"And although I'm certain Wallace doesn't have any reservations with sharing his findings, I believe he's under direct orders from the sheriff not to confer with me about this case."

"It's not a case. Did he offer any information?"

"No," she sighed, rubbing her hands together. The sunlight behind her snapped brilliantly against the snow and caught in her silver hair. "But he did tell me that Broghin is at this moment on his way here to talk to you."

"To me?" That one tagged me hard. "Why?"

"I'm not certain, but Wallace claims that Broghin is in, quote, a sour enough mood to piss lemonade, unquote."

"Oh, that's just terrific." I had a feeling I was going to be heading to jail again soon.

"He has a flair for capturing the spirit of the sheriff, our Keaton Wallace does. I believe we may have to continue mending a few pickets on those neighborly fences."

"But what did I do?"

No point in asking; there didn't have to be a particular reason behind Broghin pissing lemonade or wanting to heave me off a bridge. I'd known him my whole life, but the first time we ran into each other in a collision-course was a week after my parents died in a car accident out at the Turnpike, on their way to visit me during my senior year at New York University. Anna had gone along; on the day I nearly cracked Broghin's skull, she was still in a coma, her spine having been crushed in the wreck.

I was as alone in my life at that moment as

I can imagine myself ever being.

Broghin didn't take kindly to my pestering him during his investigation of the accident, and took even less kindly to my hurling his desk chair at him when he wrote the crash off as Dad's fault, claiming the autopsy had found enough liquor in my father's stomach that it was a miracle he ever backed out of the driveway. They said he'd fallen off the wagon after seven years of Alcoholics Anonymous; once a drunk, always a drunk.

When I was released from jail three months later Anna had come out of her coma. Maybe we both felt a little like we were being reborn together, with the rest of our family gone, and the two of us now orphaned.

She told the police about my father being forced off the road by a black sedan, and how, after a burning swirl of tearing metal the car went into a ravine, and through a haze of agony she'd seen a man climbing down the rocks. At first she thought he'd come to help, and tried with her remaining strength to attract his attention, to no avail. Thrown from the back seat and pinned beneath the overturned car, she couldn't move or even whisper — that's what had saved her life. Seconds before passing out, the truth clarified as she watched the man carefully take my mother's jaw in his hands and snap her neck. My father survived long enough for his killer to pour half a bottle of scotch down his throat.

Broghin listened to Anna's statement and re-opened his single sheet file. Whatever evidence there might have been was three months old. In my cell, I'd fumed and mulled the facts over; afterwards, you could say I wasn't the most stable person in the world as I went to hunt for reasons. I threatened to separate Wallace's gluteus from his maximus if he didn't exhume my father's body and make a toxicology report out on the amount of alcohol in his bloodstream, there hadn't been enough time for any alcohol to get into my father's system. He should have done it the first time, but Wallace is an alcoholic too and probably enjoyed believing that no one ever reformed. Perhaps I was crazy, but I cared as much about getting an apology as I did catching my parents' murderer.

Anubis barked when a police cruiser pulled up outside.

Sheriff Franklin Broghin opened the car door and shifted his considerable bulk to get out of the seat, wrestling with his gun belt. He would come up to my chin if he could ever stand close enough to do it — his eighty-pound belly forced him back a good two or three feet. He could never get nose to nose with anybody, never look anyone square in the eye.

"Let me handle this, Jonathan."

"This has somehow already gone beyond our handling. It started off that way."

She nearly grinned. "I think so, too. I wonder why that is?"

Broghin didn't even glance at the murder site as he trundled up the path. My heart started hammering and my breath hitched; whenever I saw him I could only think of the three months my father had been in the grave and shamed. Anubis locked on and perked and snarled.

"I'm not ready for this today," I said.

"Don't let your temper get away with you, dear. Let's listen to what the man has to say."

"I'll listen so long as he doesn't yell in my face and poke me in the chest." Broghin had a nasty habit of poking people in their chests. He was doing it to me, screaming about how my father was a lousy bum, when I flung his desk chair at his head.

I met him at the door, sticking my chest out like a pubescent girl, waiting for him to jab me with his frankfurter fingers. Instead of having a smirk already curling his lips, he actually gave me a friendly smile and reached out to shake my hand.

"Hello, Johnny, nice to see you're back for a little visit. It's been a while since the last time. You should come on home more often."

"Ah," I wanly replied, "okay." I stepped out of his path as he took off his coat and approached my grandmother. Anubis stood without a sound and glared. The dog was always one word away from killing someone.

"Keep that damn animal away from me, Anna. You know he's just waiting for the right moment to tear my yahoos off."

Yahoos? I decided my grandmother never had an affair with Broghin. Forgetting all the other jerkwater town close-mindedness he'd exemplified over the years, it simply wasn't acceptable that Anna would go to bed with a man who actually used such a word as *yahoos* to describe any part of his anatomy.

She pulled Anubis aside while Broghin leaned down and hugged her, cautiously working his way around the coffee table to the couch, careful of his yahoos. He didn't sit down so much as he quit fighting gravity and let himself topple backwards to the cushions. The couch slid a few inches and thumped the wall, shaking the picture frames.

Anna turned her chair and smiled at me as if to say, *Now what?* I smiled stupidly back at her. She asked, "Franklin, may I offer you a cup of tea or coffee? We have a good deal of food left over from brunch. I can fix you a plate."

"No," the sheriff said. "Thanks anyway. I was just paying a call to see how you were, after last night."

"You needn't have worried. I'm fine."

"Yeah, I knew you would be." He nodded in my direction. "But I'm still glad Johnny's here with you. You're on your own too much of the time as it is, and you really shouldn't be alone after something like this, Anna. I feel a lot better knowing there's somebody else with you for at least a few days."

It was obvious she didn't want to hear him talk about being watched over and taken care of, which only served to remind her of her own fears; the night had already faded before the fervor of her curiosity. "Have you made any progress in the case?"

"Not a whole hell of a lot, Anna, to be truthful," he said. Broghin had a deep, melodic and pillowy voice when he wasn't shouting, along the lines of Bing Crosby. "Harraday was a creep from a whole family

51

of creeps and I guess it just caught up with him is all."

"Caught up with him?"

"Yup."

Anna waited for him to explain himself. When he didn't she commented, "I fail to catch your meaning."

"What meaning?"

"Your meaning."

"My meaning? What I mean?" The pulse in Broghin's neck ticked rapidly and the snow left a sheen of droplets on his face. "Well, it's the same old story. You've got a kid who's a bum and is always going to be a bum. He gets into trouble as a teenager and works his way into the fringes of serious crime. He steals a couple cars when he's bored, snatches a few purses, burgles houses every now and again, and eventually makes a few enemies. He was probably moving up to committing heavy-time felonies when he came across an even worse badass who double-crossed him. A drug deal gone wrong is my guess."

I said, "Lowell told me that Margaret's home was Harraday's first burglary."

"First one we caught him at, Johnny. That doesn't mean it was his only one." He pointed his index finger at me and cocked his thumb, shooting me with a silly grin like an oversized uncle playing games with his favorite nephew. It knotted my stomach to see him act this way. I almost would've preferred the red-faced maniac who'd cuffed me and escorted me to jail.

Jesus, I thought, Broghin's nervous about something, too. What the hell is going on?

Anna asked, "What was the cause of Richie Harraday's death, Franklin?"

"I'd rather not say."

"Why is that?"

"I'd rather not say why not."

"Why not?" she asked.

"Why I don't want to tell you? Because I don't want to, Anna."

"Yes, but why is that?" she insisted. It cracked me up how she worked him.

"Why? Because we're so early into this investigation — Christ, it's barely been twelve hours — and I don't want to start taking potshots in the dark. We need more to go on." He held his hand up as if to ward her off. "When we have some leads I'll let you know exactly what's happening, but for now let me handle it."

"But surely telling me the cause of death is not taking a potshot in the dark if Wallace has already finished his medical examination."

"No, it's not," Broghin consented, "but

this is a homicide and we don't want to run around bouncing into walls. Besides, they're only preliminary results."

It was a pleasure to see my grandmother hitting her stride, as tenacious as the rotweiller. She wasn't going to let go of this one until she got the answers. I even felt a bit sorry for Broghin because, for whatever reason, he was trying so hard to be a nice guy.

"I can appreciate your feelings, my friend, but with deepest sincerity I can promise you that I will not —"

"You won't anything," he told her, "because you're going to stay at home and read your books and cook for your grandson and not get in my hair this time, Anna."

I did not point out that he only had nine or ten hairs on his head.

"I have no intention of interfering with any police matters."

"No, not you," he said.

"Not us," I said.

Anna checked her Christie collection and found further resolve. She wheeled closer. "But you cannot argue that I do have a certain amount of personal involvement, and I am naturally curious to know as much as possible about the events that have transpired on my property. I believe it is my right to know."

Broghin groaned. "I —"

"Or is it that you find me incapable of accepting the truth because of some notion that I am merely an elderly woman who should be watching soap operas and knitting baby booties?"

"No," Broghin said. "No, nothing like that."

Of course not, and she knew it, but she was leading him into an argument when there was nothing to argue about, the same as she'd done to me on the phone last night. Backing off from that dead end, she cut through the repartee and asked an outright question. "Did Harraday die from a broken neck?"

"No."

"Was his murder premeditated or —"

"Goddammit!" the sheriff shouted, and it did me good to see he remained the same man beneath his newfound veneer of soft-spokenness. "I knew you'd start giving me the third degree the minute I set foot in here. Why is it that you never let me do my job without running me through your gamut of inquisitiveness?"

"Oh my," Anna said, and burst out laughing. "Gamut of inquisitiveness. That's very nice. Oh, I enjoy that immensely, Franklin. That's a fine effort. Gamut of inquisitiveness."

"C'mon, give me a break."

"I am merely trying to understand our current situation. It may be your job, but it might very well be my life."

Broghin frowned and couldn't meet her eye. He had a hard time figuring out where to set his gaze and decided the dog's water dish was as good as any. "He died of natural causes."

"And what naturally caused him to slam-dunk himself into a garbage can?" I asked.

"I believe the sheriff meant he died an accidental death of sorts."

"Yup, it was an overdose."

"I see," Anna said. "Of what?"

"What difference does that make?"

"It could make a world of difference, as you already know, Franklin."

"Alcohol and barbiturates and cocaine," he admitted. "That's why I said it was a drug deal that went bad. He and his partner were probably trashing themselves and it got out of hand. Harraday overdosed and the other guy panicked and dumped the body. It only makes sense."

Anna's gaze caught mine.

"No," I said. "I don't think it does. Why would someone party with cocaine only to undermine it with the come-down effects of barbiturates? It doesn't seem like he'd do it in one sitting, anyway."

Broghin tried shifting to face me and couldn't quite heave himself around. "Not usually, but it happens. Listen you. Just stay put and don't go running around town trying to play cop."

"Somebody has to."

He went, "Hemphh" as though he'd caught an uppercut.

It was the wrong thing for me to say, and I knew it when I said it. Broghin's Bing Crosby quality went diving out the window. Now he sounded more like Ethel Merman. "You just let me handle this! You get in my way and I swear I'll throw your ass back in jail and keep you there until your social security checks come in!"

"You don't want me to run my gamut of inquisitiveness?"

Broghin's lips puffed into bloodless leeches. He hefted himself to his feet in a jumble of chins and spare tires and stuff clinking on his gun belt. "You think I'm kidding?"

"No."

Anna rolled the chair between me and the sheriff, her hands out in a placating manner. "Thank you for stopping by, Franklin. I value your judgment."

"Like hell you do, Anna!" He looked like

Costello at the end of the Who's On First? routine. "You two are the most infuriating people I've ever met. Get this through your thick Kendrick skulls in case you're thinking of wandering around Felicity Grove with nothing better to do than pester the police and get into trouble — stay clear!" Anubis stood and eyed Broghin's yahoos as the sheriff grabbed his coat and bee-lined out the door.

"How adorably sweet that man can be," Anna said. "He fears for my life."

"Yes."

"I believe it's time we attempted to discover exactly what it is we've been caught in the middle of, Jon."

"Good idea," I said.

In the back of my mind I wondered what our second faux pas was going to be like.

5

That night I dreamed of making love to Michelle, which wasn't as strange as it might seem. Or maybe it was, but by now could be expected. Whenever I meet a new woman I'm attracted to she goes directly into my subconscious and winds up stirring a lot of silt.

I met Michelle in my senior year of college when I returned to finish school after finding my parents' killer. She and I both happened to take a course on the unlikely subject of *Dadaism and French Surrealistic Poetry*. Needless to say, the class was canceled due to lack of enrollment, and Michelle and I wound up in line together at the registrar's office for three hours, trying to change our schedules.

A couple of movies and dinners later and we were more than friends and occasional lovers; it kept on that way for most of the spring semester, right into our final weeks at the university, when we rapidly became more serious. She was a lifeline I held on to more tightly than I would have under different circumstances, and she was an orphan who liked the idea of having someone to take care of her after having to look out for herself for so long. I proved to be a composite father, mother, brother, and child figure, as well as her husband. Our marriage came shrieking like a newborn out of misplaced needs and wants.

But needs and wants count. We lasted longer than we should have, more than two years. During that time I don't think we ever had so much as a fight, which only served to confirm that we didn't really give a damn what the other was doing. I opened the bookshop in the Village with the money I'd inherited, and Michelle worked as an aerobics instructor until she realized she could make a mint stripping at one of the Manhattan clubs that regularly featured porno stars and ladies who took baths in big tubs of champagne. Even that didn't bother me so much as her getting dropped off at five in the morning on the back of motorcycles driven by guys named Viper and Noose, the skin of her shoulders and breasts slowly filling with tattoos of dragons, orchids, and Iron Crosses. When she started getting tattoos of other men's names along her inner thigh, it was pretty obvious our marriage had come to an end and at least one of us should take heed.

The only emotional baggage I still carry around is my resentment that she doesn't call me more often at four in the morning.

I lounged in bed for an hour, writing scurrilous notes and making lists. I underlined Margaret's, Richie's, and Anna's names and circled them over and over, drawing arrows between them with big question marks across the page. Philip Marlowe had nothing on me. In the light of morning, I wasn't quite as sure as I had been last night that we had anything here. Even my suspicions about Richie's OD. hadn't held up through the night. Broghin had been right — when you're partying, you'll take anything you can get your hands on: quaaludes, amphetamines, coke, crack, even LSD and heroin were making comebacks in the City, giving cocaine a run for its money as the selected drug of stressed-out Yuppies.

Nothing came easily, there was no sense to be made like this. I finally tore out the page and threw the crumpled ball in the trash.

I called the shop and spoke with my assistant Debi Kiko Mashima, a twenty-year-old NYU student who is probably the most brilliant person I've ever met, except for the fact that she's never realized that she could find much better employment just about anywhere else. As a second generation Japanese, she'd caught the best of both worlds: the hard-drive studying learned under the tutelage of her family, and a breezy hipness and sense of humor she'd picked up on the streets. Only her love for books keeps her with me, which is fine, because I'll be at a tremendous loss when she graduates. She's one of those people whose smile is so infectious that her glow of cheerfulness rubs against you like an affectionate cat.

"Hey, Boss!" Debi said. "What's happening up in Felicitous Grove?"

"You mean excluding the broken body in the trash, the freaked-out sheriff, crazy Mr. Crummler and his hordes of demons and ghosts, and a new woman to whom I may soon pledge my undying love?"

"Yeah, excluding all that. You doing anything?"

"Nothing much."

Debi's airy laugh made me chuckle. "You'll have to fill me in when you get back."

"Will do. And thanks for working the overtime."

"No problem at pay and a half, Boss."

"We never discussed pay and a half."

"Oooh, and now is such a bad time, what

with you being in such a clinch at this time, eh?"

Debi had finally smartened up to this whole employment thing. "You win, of course. I hope the extra hours aren't cutting into your classes or affecting your love life too much."

"Nah," she said. "Me and my boyfriend Chuck do it right in back of the shop. The Brontë sisters turn him on."

"Me, too."

Again the laughter, but when she was done she slashed straight to the bone. Her lively tone sobered in a heartbeat and she said, "Be careful, Boss."

"Deb, you've been working with me for six months and no matter how many times I've asked you to stop calling me Boss, you still do. It makes me feel like a mafioso."

"What can I say? You remind me of Bruce Springsteen. Gotta go, Boss, those German sellers are here and I've —"

"What? They're in New York now?"

"Yeah, we're having coffee. A husband and wife team, been in the book trade since before Il Duce and the housepainter planned to take over the world. We're talking ancient, but really nice people. Apparently it was a last minute arrangement to mix business with pleasure and come visit their great-granddaughter, who works in the fashion district. But don't worry, I've got it under control. They've been telling me about the wall coming down, like it happened this morning. We're going to lunch and work out a deal for several more books."

"Two important words, Deb: currency conversion. Don't get screwed around on it."

She threw on a Japanese accent. "Ah so, tank'a vewwy much. Kiko no undastand concept'a papah money. Kiko sit all day paint face for Kibuki tonight. Tank'a vewwy much."

"Hey, I can't afford . . ."

"Relax, you'll love it. I think I can get us a couple of first editions of Grass' *Headbirths* and *Cat and Mouse*, too. There's a guy on the Upper East Side willing to pay bucks for them."

"The couple speak English?" I asked.

"No, I'm fluent in German. Didn't I ever tell you that? Japanese, too. Maybe it has something to do with the war. And hey, remember me when I want an unscheduled night off."

"You got it."

"*Auf Wiedersehen,* Boss."

I hung up and went downstairs. Anubis

wandered over and slurped my hand, then stalked back to Anna. She sat beside her reading table finishing up the Christie novel, another book already laid out and waiting to replace *Sleeping Murder*. "How many times have you read that?" I asked.

"Three. I sometimes wonder if she did not make her villains too appealing. I enjoy them all quite a lot, even when they're unmasked as the murderers. And then I hate to see them foiled."

"I'm like that with Elmore Leonard. His bad guys are often hipper than the heroes."

"You look refreshed," she said. "Did you sleep well?"

"Yes."

"Good. Breakfast is in the kitchen."

She had made another feast exactly as yesterday's even though there was still enough leftover food in the refrigerator to feed Peoria. "Anna, you're overcooking like mad. Don't bother with this every day."

"But I enjoy it, dear."

Each of us collected our thoughts and turned them over, waiting for pieces to click and hoping for bolts of inspiration and enlightenment. My grandmother has the ultimate poker face, like a Himalayan lama who had total control over each facial muscle, every tic and nuance.

Eventually she broke the silence. "I am going to pay a visit to the owner of the pawnshop. Perhaps Margaret's jewelry had genuine value and she was murdered for it, and then Richie in turn." She didn't seem convinced it was the proper tack to take, but realized a thread had to be pulled before any of the tapestry could unravel. "It's a long shot I'd like to follow up on. What are your plans?"

"I don't know," I said, thinking about my rotten list.

"You could ask Lowell for more information about Richie's dealings with the criminal element."

"Anna, only you could make a car thief sound like Moriarity."

She shrugged and tossed the book aside. No helpful hints from Dame Agatha this morning. "Well then, you'll think of something."

"Drop me off in town and I'll rent a truck from Edelman's Garage."

"A truck?"

"Yeah. I'm going to drive up into the back hills. I think I'll go see Maurice Harraday."

"Be careful," she said as she resumed reading. "And remember to call him Tons."

After I picked up a '78 Jeep with a cracked

66

windshield, no heater, and a smashed back bumper from Duke Edelman, I followed my grandmother's advice and went to see Lowell. He sat behind his desk at the police station, talking on the phone while tapping out his frustration with a pencil. I took the opportunity to use his coffeemaker to grab myself a cup while he calmly spoke to a woman who wanted him to arrest her husband's friends for keeping him out until three o'clock in the morning, and him with his allergies.

Across the hall, Broghin's door was open but he wasn't in his office. When Lowell had finished explaining a vast amount of constitutional law to the woman, he hung up and said, "Let's go for a drive."

"You don't sound happy."

"That's a rare state of being for me lately."

"We headed anywhere in particular?"

"C'mon."

Uptight, his manners were mechanical, back straight enough to surf on as we walked to his cruiser. I fed off his bad mood and fell back into funk, wishing the tulips would arrive today. We drove past the courthouse, then over to the high school where we circled the ice-encrusted football field. He refused to talk, and the solid frustration that had been growing in my chest shifted into the steady beat of annoyance. Still, I kept my mouth shut because we were basically doing the same thing we had done two days ago when he picked me up from the airport.

Another ten minutes passed, blinding slashes of light reflecting off the snow of last night as we drove by the lumber yard, power station and movie theater, before Lowell scratched his beard stubble and said, "I think Richie's killer left a note."

"Okay."

"Now the question."

"So where is it?"

"Uh huh."

My stomach filled with the warm ebb of blood and nausea. Muscles in my neck bunched tight, and the hair on my nape pricked like quills. On top of that, the anger turned too, into rage, because Lowell shouldn't have wasted the twenty minutes before he told me. "What makes you think so?"

"That night," he began and dragged up short. "That night I searched the yard to make sure the perp was gone. Broghin stayed with the body. Anna and Jim Witherton came out onto the porch, and the sheriff kept telling them to go inside and stay in the house. When I got back I noticed a dry spot on Richie's pants leg."

"As if something had been covering it while the snow came down."

"Yeah."

"Is that it?"

"This morning I walked in on Broghin and he was folding up a water-stained piece of paper, you could see that ink had run. It made a connection, not much of one, but I guess it showed because he threw it in a drawer like a boy caught with his father's *Playboy*. That meant a whole lot more." He slowed for a red light. A couple holding hands, pushing a stroller, stepped into the crosswalk. "I've been on this job for eight years and I thought I'd seen that man in just about every mood there is. Happy as a kid at Christmas, proud, vengeful, even throwing up on himself. But I've never actually seen him *rattled*."

"Anna can do it to him easily. I want her protected."

"I don't think the note was for her."

"Why?"

"Because Broghin can be a jerk but he's still a good sheriff. If he thought she was in any kind of danger he would have had me or one of the other boys watching over her around the clock."

"So you say."

"It's the truth, and you know it, Jon."

I wasn't certain what I knew anymore, except that I didn't know as much as I needed to; we drove around the park, nostalgia trying to work into my system and utterly failing. Felicity Grove wasn't as retrograde as I'd come to believe, and it lost more of its sleepy, peaceful milieu all the time — it seemed the town had caught up fast with the insanity of the cities. What was going to come next?

"You think maybe he or his family was threatened?" I asked.

"Yeah, I do." The world was being squeezed through his Clint Eastwood squint. "The sheriff's been on edge for two days. He barks at the people he's usually nice to and he's a genuine doll to everybody he always screams at."

"I noticed. He actually called me Johnny."

Lowell shook his head. "He's twisted ass over backwards, and the only thing that can do that is for something to prod the man where he breathes."

"I promised not to get in the way and obstruct justice on this one if I could help it, but if you think that Broghin himself is hiding evidence . . . ?"

"I didn't say that."

"No, but you came perilously close."

"I know you don't get along with the man,

70

and I can't say I blame you. You just think of him as a butterball who razzes you too much, but I've seen him put his life on the line. Whatever the hell is eating at him, I've got to give him time to work it out."

"Why are you telling me this?" I said, staring out the window so I wouldn't have to look at him. "You know I'm not going to let it lie."

He reached out and touched my arm gently, with his wrist hanging over my shoulder, the way we had posed for our football team yearbook pictures. I didn't like this pull of the past. "Because I'm asking you to let it lie."

My turn to be in charge of the silence. We drove back to the police station and he pulled up in front of the Jeep. We sat there for another few minutes, watching the traffic lights change, people walking by. Between us, the shotgun's presence was disturbing and comforting.

"Okay, Lowell," I said. "I'll let you run with it for now. I'll give Broghin the benefit of the doubt, but only for so long." We got out of the car. "If what he's hiding has anything to do with Anna I'm going to find out. And then there'll be hell *and me* to pay."

"Good line," he said. "I like that. You're

going to have knees knocking from here to Jacksonville."

I drove up to the back hills, a sort of mystical area of the county where the structures of town faded away to sprawling copses and scattershot cabins and trailers. The ragged timberline took over the landscape. I lost control of the Jeep twice on the unpaved roads and nearly skidded off the mountain. Although here was an intoxicating natural beauty, this wasn't friendly country in the winter. If I didn't gather my concentration I might wind up as bad off as Richie.

It wasn't that stupid a line, I thought. Pretty awful all right, but not as bad as 'gamut of inquisitiveness' anyway.

When I got in the general vicinity of Tons Harraday's home I stopped at a two-pump gas station and asked directions. Turns out I wasn't in the general vicinity after all — Harraday lived to the east of Warner fork, where the peak of the hills met the river as the waters curved south along the grade, washing down into the valley. There weren't many road signs; some had been blown down in the storm, and some were probably still standing but invisible in the snow. The rest had been shot to pieces. I made a few more mistakes, the worst of which was when

I followed a muddy trail to a dead end and had to drive a half mile in reverse back to the main road because the path was too narrow to turn around on.

Finally I spotted a mailbox someone had dug free from the snow: MILNER. I kept going another quarter mile to the next place. The mailbox there stood covered by layers of ice, which served to magnify the name: HARRADAY. I pulled up and parked at the bottom of a long, partially graveled driveway with only a single tire track cutting across the ground. Tons rode a motorcycle, even in winter.

Though it was more than a mile away, I could clearly hear the chops of the river. Broghin had said Richie Harraday was a creep from a long line of creeps; that could be true, but apparently Harraday's father at least had once been a logger. Lumberjack houses had the same general structure to them: mostly brick and mortar, with stone foundations, as if knowing how easy it was to cut down wood they set themselves inside homes with more permanence. Off to one side of the house a trailer sat on cinder blocks, like a newly added room slapped onto the cramped quarters.

Before I could start for the house I heard the rough sound of running behind me, chunks of snow kicking up. I spun and two Dobermans that had never had their ears pinched stopped on a dime and stared at me without emotion. They didn't growl or bark or advance, and their nubby tails didn't wag in the slightest. They looked odd without their ears pointed, a tad friendlier maybe, but their yellow eyes gave multitudes of reasons why Dobermans are not man's best friend. They're also just about the only breed of dog that can look completely ferocious without baring their fangs. Not even Anubis can do that.

These two were brothers, a team, standing equidistant from my left and right sides, fifteen feet away. I did my best not to swallow, blink, or breathe. All three of us were very good at playing statue and we stayed like that for a good three or four minutes, which, relatively speaking, seemed like an hour's worth of real time. If I ran I wouldn't even make it to the Jeep.

Cripes, didn't anybody own poodles or basset hounds anymore?

Another two or three minutes passed and I was getting tired and cold; I lifted my foot up to take a step and they both began to growl. I put my foot back on the ground very carefully and decided I wasn't really that tired or cold.

A large man wearing a ripped, red flannel shirt and a leather vest came out of the house and casually walked up behind the Dobermans. The dogs didn't turn, their gazes nailed on me. I felt the ridiculous urge to shriek *yahoos!* and cover my crotch.

He let me stew a while longer, enjoying himself. He stood at least six foot five, muscular, but with a fair amount of fat around the middle, built for the mountains. He had tiny features scrunched into the center of a wide face and a well-trimmed beard.

Sweat rolled down my spine and made me itch like hell. He lit a cigarette and said quietly, "I suppose you got a reason for sneakin' around my property."

"I wasn't sneaking." At the sound of my voice the Dobermans inched closer.

"Fred and Barney made sure of that."

"Are you Tons Harraday?"

"Yeah," he said. "Who're you?"

I told him my name and my reason for being here; I did it without moving my lips and put Edgar Bergen to shame. The story was strange and involving, and explaining it to Tons was like making my lists again, coming up short with limited information. I edited the bit about the sheriff holding back the scrap of paper. I didn't want to start a war unless I knew which side I should be on.

Somewhere in there I mentioned how sorry I was that his brother was dead; he nodded and looked me in the eye as if searching for lies.

"Can I move now?" I asked.

"You carry a gun or a knife?"

"No."

"You ought to. Every man ought to." Tons slapped his thigh and the dogs ran in circles at his feet, then he petted them and yelled, "Go on. Go, get." They darted off in the direction they'd originally come.

"I recognize your name," he said. "You're the one who helped out the DeGrase family last year, right? Helped the cops find the kid?"

I nodded. "That's right."

"Goddamn cops can't do shit."

I nodded more. I thought it was best to show a man who was six inches taller than me that we were of similar minds.

"And now you're looking out for your grandmother?"

"Yeah."

"I can understand that," he said. "But I'll tell you, Richie didn't kill the flower lady." Tons kicked at the snow and planted his feet firmly. "Believe me, my brother couldn't hurt nobody, and I mean nobody. He was a good kid, but more than that, he didn't have the guts for it. He could be a real jerk, too, but mostly 'cause he was young." He stared somewhere over my left shoulder. "We used to go fishing. I don't even know why he broke into the lady's house for a lousy coupla bucks."

"Did he mention it to you?"

"Not a word."

"Did he have a partner?"

"For what?" Tons said. "He never really did anything. He went for a joyride or two, but I wouldn't consider that even stealin' a car. He never kept any, didn't chop 'em and sell 'em for parts."

"What about the drugs?"

He grunted. "Everybody does a little now and then. Richie liked coke, but he never did enough to kill himself. It was a set-up. Somebody poisoned him."

"Why?"

"If I knew that they'd be dead."

"Was he hanging around with anybody in particular? New buddies? Some rougher types?"

"Roughest Richie ever saw was me, and I taught him to stay away from my type." He was proud of that fact and proffered a grin.

"A girlfriend?"

"Nah," he said, but after a pause added, "I mean, he could've had a girl on the side. He liked to stay out late and kept his trap shut on where he'd been, but Richie was . . . he was kinda scared of women. Shy, really, when you get down to it. A quiet kid, he kept to himself." He spoke slowly, remembering his younger brother. "Too much, I think. That's what got him into . . . trouble." The final word fell out of his mouth with a thud, too hollow a word to express his grief. "He didn't do much. We liked to go fishing." He licked his lips and crossed his arms and spat on the ground. When he looked at me again I could see he was a man who could cage his emotions like dogs and let them out one at a time. Vengeance burned. I knew the feeling. "I want the bastard who murdered my brother. Richie had a long ways to go, but he would've learned. He would've learned."

"Do you know if —"

A woman's high-pitched shout cut off my question. "Honey!"

"Yeah!" he called back without turning.

Harraday's wife — the girl who Lowell said had settled Tons down — stood in the doorway of the house holding a blanket-wrapped infant in her arms. She couldn't have been much older than twenty, with unnaturally scarlet hair that wafted around her shoulders. Her nose was too long, lips crooked and cheeks too high, but her dark eyes overshadowed the slight imperfections and made the rest of her face appealing. She had an energy about her. She glanced at and dismissed me in the same second. The baby started crying.

"Come in and eat."

"Please, Deena, I'm talking out here. I'll be there in a minute."

"I've got to go to work," she said.

"I know, babe. Just give me a coupla seconds, all right?"

"It's your supper. I don't have time to change her so you'll have to do it." She let the door slam.

"You through?" Tons asked.

"I've got a few more questions."

"Yeah, well, I got some of my own." He tried to figure my angle, deciding whether or not I could be trusted. Maybe he thought I had something to do with Richie's murder. "Whyn't you meet me at Raimi's tonight."

"Who's Raimi?" I asked.

"Raimi's Pub. It's out by the Turnpike on Crane Avenue, right over the tracks. Know where that is?"

"Yeah."

"I'll see you there around ten. That okay?"

"Fine."

I got back to the Jeep without seeing the Dobermans and threw it into Drive. I became overly aware of the scar tissue above my kidneys. Six years ago Raimi's had a different name. It had been Jackals then. I hadn't stepped foot inside the place since the day I was shot.

6

I took a ride past the flower shop, but Katie had a sign on the door that read BACK AT and showed a little clock when she'd return. I couldn't make out the time and decided to visit early tomorrow.

In the morgue parking lot I spotted Anna's van. I pulled over a few spaces down and decided to wait outside rather than walk into Wallace's office and put him even more on the spot.

The morgue had been designed to be a morgue and you'd never think it was anything else; the front of the place was slate and stone, giving it the elemental look of rock, freezing and dire and fundamental as death. It wasn't eerie, just ugly.

I listened to the radio, hearing songs that are tired everywhere else, but, remarkably enough, in Felicity Grove they still had a bit of life left to them. I couldn't have stomached the like of Meatloaf's "Two Out of Three Ain't Bad" if I didn't have snow on the ground and the heavy scent of pine to remind me of a time when girls used to bring their AM radios to the park and watch us play football in the mud.

It was either that or think about the note, and whenever I thought of the scrap of paper Broghin had snatched off Richie Harraday's body, of what it might explain or threaten or demand, of what he was hiding and denying, my nerves started to crawl.

For fifteen minutes I tapped the steering wheel in time with other such classics as "Staying Alive" and "The Piña Colada Song," until the building's metal doors swung open with a jarring screech. Keaton Wallace pushed my grandmother in her wheelchair, the two of them speaking animatedly. Wallace had difficulty getting the smaller front tires over the single step out front, but with a little careful maneuvering, rolling backwards and sideways until the wheels aligned, they managed. Anna said something and Wallace stopped to lift his head and give out with a couple throaty guffaws as they came down the long walkway to the curb.

In his mid-fifties, Wallace was buoyant with a childish quality that didn't go with the barbershop quartet haircut and bristly peppered mustache that made him look like Teddy Roosevelt. He grinned too much because his dentures didn't fit correctly, and he could fool you with his charm into thinking he wasn't a complex man. The truth was that he had more sides to him than you could ever be sure of: he'd had a serious mean streak until his wife left him a decade ago, and I hadn't heard him raise his voice since he remarried a woman half his age; he'd been in AA with my father for years, and hadn't only fallen off the wagon a few times, but hijacked the sucker straight to a couple of winery tours.

Maybe I should've said hello to him, but I was afraid he might feel under the gun, with me waiting for the two of them like this. I slunk lower in my seat and caught the tail end of their conversation as Wallace helped Anna into the van's lift. He was saying: ". . . and don't let the trouble with Timmons bring you down. He's a selfish, cantankerous fool who cares more about the dollar than he does his own kids, but he'll have to comply with city ordinances."

She nodded. "Thank you again, Keaton. I appreciate your taking the time to speak with me."

"Oh, knock it off. I was only in the middle of —"

"Please. I'd prefer not to know who or what was under that sheet."

Wallace laughed. "I really do enjoy seeing

you, Anna. I just wish for once we could get together under different circumstances."

"I do, as well, and I hope when I pass on you don't insult my memory by covering me over with linen from the JC Penney's Catalogue."

"You'll outlive me, my sweet," he said. "And while you're offering prayers and crying your eyes out, make sure that dog of yours doesn't piddle on my grave."

"I would say we have a mutual understanding then."

He kissed her on the cheek as she rose on the lift. "You should drop by the house more often, Anna. Come over anytime you like. In fact, maybe you, Vera, and I can go to a movie or take in a show. She's dying to see *Les Miserables*. Only thing is it's touring in Toronto."

"That's more than a four-hour drive. You may as well go to Manhattan. Broadway is nearly as close."

"But with the pain in the ass traffic and parking and the damn subways at night, I'd prefer Toronto. At least I won't have to put a 'No Radio' sign in the back window of the wagon." Wallace dropped back a step and stared at his feet, a surefire sign he was about to change the subject. "After all these years I think I'm actually beginning to accept your . . ." — he took his time coming up with the right word — "inclinations into such matters."

My grandmother made a pshaaww gesture. "I doubt that's entirely true, my friend, but thank you for saying it."

"Just don't tell the Sheriff I let you see the file. That's all I need is for him to start parading around, moaning and breaking my chops."

"My lips are sealed, even under threat of torture."

He grew concerned. "Trust me on this then. Listen to me for once, will you? Don't let that grandson of yours get in over his head, searching for clues and villains and conspiracies that don't exist."

"And if they do?"

"Then that's even more reason to get him to back off. But I'm telling you that that boy's body being found on your lawn was just a fluke; it had nothing to do with you personally."

"I certainly do hope it wasn't personal. However, we have no way of knowing whether it was merely a fluke. Not yet."

"The police will have this matter resolved shortly."

"The case will be solved, yes," she said. "Once again, Keaton, thank you."

Wallace turned and re-entered the morgue, the door slamming home behind him. Anna started the van and began to pull away before she saw me coming. I got in beside her, waiting for the engine to warm because the heater in the Jeep didn't work and most of my blood had congealed.

"What trouble?" I asked.

She waved me off. "You shouldn't eavesdrop, Jonathan. Goodness, your nose is burning red. How long have you been hovering in the shadows?"

"What trouble?"

"I am perfectly capable of handling my own problems. Did you learn anything more from Tons Harraday?"

"No, but I'm meeting him tonight. What problems?"

"Please don't concern yourself."

"I won't so long as you tell me what happened."

"It was nothing, dear."

"I can hang in there with you on this one, Anna. The more you say things like that the more circular this conversation becomes but I can keep at it as long as you can. So just tell me already."

She gave up because she knew that in our family nobody got any rest until we knew the other's business. "Mr. Timmons is erecting a second convenience store downtown, and from what I can gather, the doorways are as equally narrow as those in his other shop, which was built long before national laws were passed allowing access to the physically disabled. I merely pointed out that he should comply with building codes."

"Oh. And he got huffy?"

"A tad, but it really was nothing." With her nose in the air she dismissed the matter. "Now, if you'll let me I'll tell you what I learned at the pawn shop." The heat came up and I began to thaw. "The proprietor, Samuel Harker, told me that Margaret's lockets were hardly worth anything at all. She paid thirty-five dollars for the pair. It certainly was not the kind of loot a more professional burglar would have immediately grabbed."

"Well, we already know he wasn't a professional, and we don't know if he grabbed them immediately. Who pawned the pieces in the first place?"

She glanced at the traffic and said, "Why don't we discuss this further at home?"

"I still have some things to do here. Just give me a wrap and we'll see what fits together later."

That suited her fine, and she readjusted

herself in the chair. I could see the intensity in her manner, the thrill of pulling the first thread that might unravel a mystery. "For obvious reasons Harker disliked giving me the name, but I eventually persuaded him. He finally admitted that they belonged to his late mother."

"He sold his Mommy's jewelry?" That gave me a creepy feeling.

"As Harker explained, she died three years ago and the lockets remained in his store until Margaret bought them. When she brought them back to have them engraved, he was delighted she cared about them so much. That's why he so easily recognized the lockets when Richie turned up with them. Besides recognizing his own engraving, he knew the jewelry had formerly belonged to his mother."

"He should have said so in the beginning. Who's got them now?"

She plucked at her chin. "That's a good question, one I never thought to ask. They weren't on Richie's person when his body was discovered. I don't know how thorough a search was made of his premises."

"No one would have cared much after the fact. Even if Richie had been guilty of the watchamacallit —"

"Felony Murder Doctrine."

"— the cops couldn't pin it on a dead man."

Curves presented themselves, and I could see how intrigued Anna had become, her imagination taking over and propelling her to Agatha Christie heights of deception and puzzles. "Perhaps Richie Harraday was merely a fall guy."

"To take the rap for murdering Margaret while robbing her house?"

"It is a possibility."

"Without leaving a mark on her? It sounds a little too convoluted. To go that far."

"It would be brilliant misdirection."

"I think we're barking up the wrong tree here. Let's use Occam's Razor and keep it simple."

"All right," she assented. "For the time being."

"You originally told me that several pieces of jewelry had been stolen. Was it only those two lockets or was more taken from Margaret's home?"

"I really don't know. I told you exactly what Deputy Lowell related to me. I haven't thought about the possibility of other stolen items since." It bothered her that I kept asking questions she didn't have answers to. "Perhaps Richie had more stashed somewhere in his house. Where are you meeting his brother tonight?"

"At some pub near the lumber trails." I didn't want to tell her it was Jackals. "Did Wallace have anything more to add to what Broghin told us last night?"

"No. He was of the same mind as the sheriff. Accidental overdose and a panicky friend who dumped the body."

"Some friend."

I opened the door and got out, then leaned against the window. "I'll be home in half an hour. I've got a few more things I'd like to check."

"What were your first impressions of Tons Harraday?"

"A nice guy," I said. "He's an animal lover."

The Corner Convenience was a kind of threshold in the lives of most fifteen year olds in Felicity Grove; my friends and I had broken our beer teeth on six-packs and cases of Genesee picked up at the store. Timmons charged us five bucks more than if we'd been old enough to buy it legally, but we paid because we didn't want the hassle and humiliation of asking adults to sneak it to us.

It wasn't far downtown, only a mile south on a block where a modest shopping center had grown around the original stores. A recently finished development of tudor homes sloped back into the blocks of Victorian houses, up a sprawl of knolls at the end of the street where ersatz oil lamp street lights lined the sidewalks. The area was a classic example of old meets new meets retro bygone days.

Unlike the jangling bells of the flower shop, The Corner Convenience had a shrill mechanical whistle that went off when you stepped on the inside rubber mat.

Timmons stood at his usual plastic-encased perch like a raven in a transparent cage, stacked high so he could see the aisles of his grocery; at the moment though he checked the cashiers' time cards, writing down numbers, mumbling to himself.

He hadn't changed in twenty years. Once a man is bald and hunched and wrinkled, he doesn't have much left to change into. Timmons must've been bald, hunched, and wrinkled since before LBJ took office. The years didn't add to or steal anything from him, they just left the crotchety, selfish, foolish man alone, wouldn't you know.

I walked over and stared at him.

He looked up. "Yeah? Can I help you?"

"Could I speak to you alone for a minute please?"

"We are alone."

I cocked a thumb behind me to the MANAGER'S OFFICE: EMPLOYEE'S ONLY down the opposite aisle. "In your office."

"Why? I can hear you just fine from here."

"I'll explain in your office."

"You will, huh?" He was suspicious, but knew me without knowing where he knew me from. "Look, I'm real busy."

"I understand. It'll only take a minute, Mr. Timmons."

He gnawed his lower lip for a moment and put down his pencil. "Make it quick, okay?" Warily, he left his roost, giving me sidelong glances, making sure I walked neither in front or behind him. For all he knew I was a health inspector or a disgruntled customer. An elderly lady in a muffler carefully looked over the vegetables to our left, squeezing them in her vein-riddled fist.

"Don't squash the tomatoes," he told her.

"I never squash the tomatoes."

"You always squash the tomatoes."

"I don't even like tomatoes. I never buy tomatoes."

We went side-by-side to his office; he unlocked it and left the door open. "Now what's this about?"

I said, "It's about a foot too narrow."

"What?"

"It's about the doorway to your new store. If it's the same as the one out front here, it's about a foot too narrow."

His eyes brightened with recognition. "You're the Kendrick kid, aren't you? Jesus. You're the one who got Mary DeGrase's baby back for her. Goddamn." The respect in his gaze lasted another five seconds before he recalled the conversation he'd had with Anna. The light dimmed and went out. He spun from me. "Well, I'll tell you the same thing I told your granny."

"I wish you wouldn't."

"You listen. This is my place, I do things my way, and if you and yours got a problem with it, then shop someplace else."

"You continue to miss the point," I said.

"She's a feisty old broad, that's for sure, and if . . ."

"Never say that about my grandmother, Mr. Timmons."

"What?"

"Never call her a broad. Especially an old one."

For a second I thought he might say something intelligent and wouldn't ask me a clichéd question; but then his prunish face sort of fell in on itself and the neolithic stupidity and anger took over. "And just what the hell are you gonna do about it if I feel like callin' her a broad or a cow or a gimp?"

"Punch you very hard in the mouth."

"Oh yeah?"

"You've a rapier wit."

"What?"

"Sit down." I pointed to the large recliner that was too big to even slide under his desk. "Sit down in your chair."

"You're threatening me," he said, astounded. "In my own goddamn place you're threatening me."

"I'm not threatening you. I'm telling you to sit down."

"You said you'd punch me in the mouth."

"That was if you called my grandmother a broad or a cow or a gimp. I never said what I'd do if you didn't sit in your chair."

The door stood open and shoppers passed by frequently; too tough to be scared, Timmons remained in his stronghold and knew something else was going on here, but he was too dense to realize what. He eyed me with that *wait'll you're on fire in the middle of the street I won't even piss on your hat* glare.

Two folding chairs were stacked behind a filing cabinet. I grabbed one and sat. "Here like this."

"You're nuts," he said, sneering now, but he sat in the recliner.

"No, with your legs closer, your feet together."

"What the hell are you doing? I'm calling the cops."

"And we'll have them investigate those ugly rumors that you've been paying off building inspectors and fooling around with your teenaged check-out girls."

Those rumors, if they did exist — and they probably did — were also probably true. Either way, it got his attention. "Who the hell's been feeding you that load of shit?"

"Now try getting out the doorway," I said. "Your office door is the same size as the front."

He didn't bother; he understood my meaning, and sneered and shook his head and the worried look faded and one of disgust replaced it. No cops, no robbery, no beating the hell out of him, just the Kendrick kid going through a big act to give a rough time about his granny's wheelchair being too big to fit inside. Like the chair he now sat in.

Someone called him over the PA, asking his assistance at the courtesy counter. The tension dissipated further and he smiled, almost amiable now, just wishing he could make me understand his point of view. "You haven't changed a thing, Kendrick. Stick to finding lost babies."

Ten o'clock spun around slowly.

Debi called during the afternoon to inform me how the deal with the German sellers went; she and her boyfriend had a great time at dinner, and she promised that the Gunter Grass books and other volumes she'd picked up were first editions in perfect condition. The exchange rate did not prove to be a problem. I knew I could move them easily and turn a quick profit, but it was seeing Debi's growing interest in the business that made her excited chatter all the more satisfying. She enjoyed being boss for a while, and that eased my conscience; I didn't know how much longer I'd be in Felicity Grove, especially if I let Lowell play out his hand and waited to confront Broghin.

I took Anubis for a walk in the park, killing time, letting him romp through the woods. By the thickets across from Anna's house, I made a half-hearted search of where Richie's murderer — if he was murdered — might have dragged his body in order to dump it. Nothing. Anubis took a hesitant step out onto the frozen surface of the pond, then another, and another, until he was in the middle and looking back, daring me to follow.

It took me twenty minutes to coax him off the ice. We went home and I tried to read but couldn't concentrate, and I didn't feel like making any more lists. At a quarter after nine I was climbing the walls and decided I'd beat Tons to the bar.

Raimi's reeked with the sweet aroma of marijuana and the cloying stink of sweat, perfume, and stale beer. Whatever the smell, it didn't seem to keep anybody away. The place thrummed, packed with a thirty-nothing crowd; the small dance floor writhed with couples pressed against each other, swaying and grinding, spilling drinks on their partners. At least the juke box wasn't spinning "The Piña Colada Song." Instead, a former local talent by the name of Zenith Brite funked out with her latest single "Calcutta By Night," vibrating the walls.

Three bartenders worked the bar, two men and a woman whose wild black hair hung in her eyes. By the time she got done serving drinks to those around me she looked like a frazzled sheep dog. Still, I got an electric smile. She swept a mass of frizzy curls off her forehead, turned her ear to me and shouted, "What can I get you?"

"Amstel Lite."

"No Amstel. We got Coors on tap, Bud, Bud Lite, Schlitz —"

"You actually sell Schlitz?"

"Yeah."

"I'll take a Bud Lite."

Whoever Raimi was, he'd upgraded the joint. Money had been poured in, and apparently that had paid off. A second bar had been set up across the room, two television screens blasted nimbus in a distant corner, and the tables in back were roomy with glass tops, rather than the scarred picnic benches of Jackals. I drank my beer and scanned the room for Tons, but couldn't make out enough faces with the vapid lighting. I moved through the crush.

It took a while, but I soon began recognizing the faces of my high school peers in the crowd: Virgil Ballard and Ralph Dawes still blocking for each other and sticking tight as they had on the football field; Luke and Shauna Chester, who'd had two sons before marrying at eighteen, then had the marriage annulled six months later only to continue dating all these years; Hazel Marris with pink, full lips that made men drop on their faces, light of my life in the eighth grade, and who would forever give my heart twinges; and Darryl Watkins, Trish Packard, Ellery Ellin, and Bill Farum and the rest of them. I spoke briefly to a few and nodded to others, grinned at Hazel when she grinned at me, but kept looking for Tons.

A hand landed on my shoulder, with a flash of glittering turquoise fingernails. "Johnny boy!"

She hugged me so ecstatically, rubbing my back, face buried against my chest so closely that I couldn't make out who she was; when she drew back I saw that Karen Bolan still had the widest say-cheese smile of any human being I've ever met. "Hey, Karen."

"Come sit, come sit! We've got a table in the back where you can hear yourself think."

"I'm meeting someone."

"Let them wait a few minutes. Come on! The gang hasn't seen you in ages!"

Nearly ten-thirty now and Tons hadn't shown.

She pulled me to a table. Karen had been loud and obnoxious in a nice sort of way trying so damn hard to get noticed; it meant she flirted with everyone in an unabashedly obvious manner, some of which carried over and earned her a rep. When she walked across a room she made sure men watched the sweet slink of her long sexy legs moving; when she laughed everybody heard the throaty squeals. She was an actress of the saddest order, one who didn't play the part so much as she let it play her.

"Willie, look who's here! Johnny Kendrick!"

Her husband, Willie Bolan, didn't mind his wife's non-stop exhibition; just to look at him you got the impression he enjoyed the rambunctious show she put on. Maybe it made him feel like other men envied him. Although he was equally outgoing and as loud as Karen, at the moment he lay sprawled as if ready for a nap. He'd been trying since he was fourteen to grow a mustache and could do little more than raise a few Fu Manchu wisps.

Karen slung herself into her seat and he rose to shake my hand. In school Willie had been a solid C student with a flair for computers, and I remembered how he'd worked with tutors to pull together for college entrance exams. The work had paid off enough for him to become one of the youngest vice presidents at Syntech. In an odd fashion, I remained moderately jealous of him.

Across from them sat Lisa and Doug Hobbes, who were the exact opposite in character to their friends; they remained glued at the hip, virtually in each other's laps, quiet, and on occasion, timid. So far as I knew, they'd been together since they were children, having grown up next door to one another: a classic example of made-for-each-other. I'd heard that Lisa had had three or four miscarriages in the last couple of years, and that they were thinking of adoption.

Willie cut through the chit-chat and went straight to the heart. "I heard a man was found dead on your property."

"Who told you that?"

He shrugged. "Everybody. You know how it works around here. What did you expect?"

"My God, it's awful," said Lisa. She was no more than four-eleven, with a voice as tiny as Tinkerbell's. I could understand how it would be difficult for her pregnancy to go full term. "Did you know the person, Jon? Anyone we would know? The police haven't released that many details."

Doug said, "And the rumor mill fills in the rest, so no one is sure exactly what happened. You've got everything from some guy with a meat cleaver in his forehead to a naked hoochie girl with a black book that can put all the pillars of the community on trial."

"No, I didn't know him," I said.

Lisa took Doug's hand and pulled it into her lap. "Was your grandmother the one to find him?"

"Jim Witherton, our next door neighbor did."

"I'd hate to think of that nice lady having to see something as hideous as that. Considering . . ."

Karen tittered happily as she struck a pose of delighted, morbid curiosity. "We heard that your grandmother's dog — what's its silly name? — that the vicious thing got to the body before the police arrived and there was hardly any meat left on the ol' boy by then."

I expected this kind of talk. "That's the rumor mill adding more gusto to the tale, Karen."

"We figured," Doug said. "It just sounded too much like what a person would make up to throw a little spice into this town. I liked the hoochie girl bit. The local stations and papers are having a field day with it, of course. All except for the *Gazette*. Family-oriented, you know."

"I wouldn't want Merlin's turkey to lose his place on the front page."

Lisa touched Doug's wrist lightly. It made me sort of claustrophobic and gave me the creeps a little to see how they were always on top of each other, petting and caressing and tugging. She frowned. "Recall what Mrs. Hollinback told us?"

"Jesus, don't remind me," he said.

"She went on for hours, literally hours, all day long at the carpet store yesterday, gossiping with anyone who slunk in the door until her puffy cheeks were blue. So excited she couldn't catch her breath for yabbering so much, alternately getting flushed and turning blue, looked like she was going to have a heart attack. People are outdoing themselves this time, saying it's everything from a serial killer to police corruption. They all want to meet Hannibal Lecter, and want him to say that line about the Falfa beans and hear him say 'Chianti.' "

"You don't show up much," Willie Bolan said, grinning. He'd learned from his wife and had a smile nearly as wide. "But when you do, you give the town a helluva perk."

"It's nice to be needed," I said.

Karen didn't like having the gore taken out of the story. "Well, I heard it straight from Mary Jean Resnick about that savage dog of yours, Johnny, and I've never known her to lie before. She heard it straight from . . ."

Willie tried to drop his cheesey smile but couldn't quite do it, trained corners of

103

mouth snapping back up. He drew his chin down and shot Karen a look. "Mary Jean Resnick is an asshole."

"Don't you dare say that, Willie!"

"What are you doing back, Jon?" Lisa asked. Her Tinkerbell voice grew even softer than usual. Not like a whisper, but low and meaningful, lips barely moving. She turned her eyes down as if ashamed of having asked. She knew what I was doing here, the only reason why I always came home.

I understood she wasn't asking a question so much as giving me a warning, hoping that for once I'd stay out of trouble. Her baby doll face turned once more to me and she worried her lips into a grimace.

"I'm meeting someone," I said.

"Hope she's got a personality," Lisa said. "I never liked that Michelle you used to bring around."

"I did, but only for a while," I said. "I'm sorry I've got to run, but this is important. It's been great seeing you all again." They responded in kind and I shook the guys' hands and hugged the ladies. Willie pinched Karen's ass and she squealed in my ear and gave him a playful slap.

I got out of there, and as I walked away Doug Hobbes said it again. "Spice."

Over the next twenty minutes I made a half dozen more circuits of the place and didn't run into Tons Harraday. Almost eleven and I was sweating and annoyed and the music gave me a headache. I decided to wait for him in the parking lot for a while, and if he didn't show by midnight I'd pay him another visit at his house, carrying a couple of steaks for his Dobermans.

Near the door, the sharp crack of breaking glass sounded to my right, and a hush fell over the immediate area. Burly hands centered on my back, shoving.

"Terrific," I grunted. This was Jackals. This would always be Jackals.

I spun and saw a short guy with a swimmer's body already in his attack stance: fists up, knees bent, snarl in place but with calm and intelligent eyes, ready to come straight on at me. Even though he had a crew cut, a collared shirt, and a tie on, he still looked like he should be named Noose or Viper. "You smacked my beer right outta my hand, boy!" he shouted.

I hadn't been anywhere near him, but I apologized quickly. There are guys itching for a chance to get into somebody else's face and run a bit of blood, and if a reason didn't come along they'd make one up. I didn't need trouble tonight. "I'm sorry," I said. "Let me buy you another."

It wasn't enough. It's rarely enough. He wasn't going to let it go. The lady bartender called, "Hey, break it up!"

"This son of a bitch knocked my beer down!" He made it sound like I'd attacked his mother with a cat-o'nine-tails.

A lot of people stared, milling around us, fascinated with the disturbance — the group mind at work. I wasn't going to fight him. Really, I thought, no matter what, I wouldn't fall into it. "Look," I said, "Let's just . . ."

The eyes should have warned me; cut through the antics and look at those beady icy baby blues. He'd already skipped the preliminary shouting match and landed a jab straight into my forehead. It hurt like hell and a blast of stars shimmied and danced, and I dropped back a few paces trying not to land on my ass. He came at me again, arms out wide like the claws of a crab, wanting to lock me up. People scattered out of our way, gasps and laughter all around. One girl shouted, "Kill him!" and I hoped she wasn't talking about me.

He jumped the last two feet between us and I pushed him off without actually hitting him. "You've got to be kidding me," I said.

Of all things, my eyebrows hurt from the punch. "An honest to God bar room brawl?"

"You . . ." he said. Most of the silly anger was gone, replaced by a well-stoked hatred.

"No, man. This is just too cliché for me."

He dipped his chin like a dog that hears a funny noise, lips compressed and almost white. I checked for the other bartenders or bouncers and didn't see any of them; Doug and Willie were on the far side of the room, and didn't even know I was involved. My other high school chums either didn't recognize me, didn't care, or liked the other guy more. "Listen," I told him. "What if we had a fight at the Lady Daphne's School of Ballroom Dancing? That'd be original, anyway. All right? Anywhere but a bar. You don't want to get in a rut."

He wasn't much for sarcasm or talking. He was, however, heavily into growling at the moment. It came from down deep where the real darkness hides. With a roar he swung at me, wide, hoping to take my head off with one shot. I sidestepped and felt the breeze of his fist pass by my chin. He was faster than he looked.

Crew cut charged and caught me low, aiming for my groin but catching me in the left thigh. It took me back a few feet before I could set myself and break his grip. He charged again and nailed me square in the stomach and I went over backward, falling hard against a window, my elbow shattering a blinking neon beer sign. In books and movies you're supposed to be able to turn an opponent's leverage against him, so when he charges you can just trip him easily and let him go slamming head first into the wall.

He grabbed a beer mug by the handle and smashed it against the bartop; it made for a competent weapon, all that jagged glass waiting to tear open a throat. I was still bewildered it had gone this far.

I dodged and backpedalled. Too slowly. He brought the mug down across my chest and I screamed, watching the blood burst from me like a leaping, crimson animal.

And so it happens.

Like the pin pulled from a grenade, it happens. You feel the rage consume you where there wasn't any an instant before; the humor flees and the wisecracks stick in your craw. The world recedes like the tide leaving corpses on the beach. Sudden clarity while the rest of the room blurs, noise stops, but the bleeding continues.

My teeth dried, and I knew I was smiling. I worked his wrist first, chopping the side of my hand down and feeling the tiny crackle of his bones beneath; he yelped and the broken mug hit the floor. I rapidly struck him in the center of his chest twice, first with my fist and then snapping down with the meaty part of my palm, two solid thumps as his breath exploded in my face. I hauled off and beat his lower ribs on the left side, then brought my knee up into exactly the same spot, and once more as he cried out a garbled curse. He got a couple of shots into my face and the sharp taste of blood filled my mouth. I kicked and swung back against his knee, jamming the cartilage the opposite way nature meant it to move. He screamed and hit a higher pitch than I've ever reached.

He ran, skipped, hobbled out the door and, shaking and ready to puke, the knot between my eyes growing and tightening, I let him go.

Somebody grabbed me from behind, turquoise fingernails again, clutching.

"I thought you were going to kill him," Karen Bolan said, excited and jubilant.

"No."

"But your eyes." Wonder in her voice, intoxication and sex. If I wasn't about to throw up it might have made me horny. "You should have seen your eyes, Johnny."

I didn't want to think about it. I didn't want to tell her that I had killed a man once, right here. He'd bought at this bar the bottle of scotch he poured down my father's throat. He was the best friend and partner of my Dad, and I'd called him Uncle Phil most of my life. He'd murdered my parents and crippled my grandmother and shot me, and even so — on that night six years ago, somewhere within the twisting child within me, while I cracked his head against the bar railing until his ears leaked — I'd almost allowed myself to cry.

"Wait'll I tell Mary Jean Resnick," Karen said.

7

I drove myself to the emergency room of County General. It took only six stitches for a silent, competent nurse to close the gash on my chest, but every time I moved too quickly the bandages pulled and pain flared. Something about Jackals wanted me dead, but I'd beaten it again.

Anna was asleep by the time I got home and I didn't wake her. Details could wait, and I still needed to talk to Tons Harraday and find out why he hadn't showed at the bar. Anubis smelled blood and disinfectant and kept making reproachful faces at me. He stalked closer, canted his head and drove his nose against my thigh, gave a discouraged grunt from the back of his throat before going off to lay in front of Anna's door.

Sleep wouldn't come for a long while, and remained only a few fitful hours. I couldn't remember any dreams, but had a vague, uneasy sense they'd been anything but as pleasant as the previous night's fantasies.

I needed a shave but didn't want to carve a greater mess out of the puffy, bruised meat that stared back at me from the mirror. My bottom lip was split and I had two purple-black eyes from the shot in the forehead. I dressed and was out of the house by eight, minutes before Anna usually got up.

The day was sunny and much warmer than earlier in the week, those vicious lake winds having died down; icicles crackled free from the telephone wires, and I passed lawns where snowmen melted into gorillas with their branch arms hanging down to the ground.

I parked in front of the flower shop, unrolled the window, and waited for Katie. The urge to see her had dug in deep for reasons I didn't fully comprehend besides the obvious. I hoped it didn't have to do with her cooking. Perhaps I wanted to talk with her so badly because she was a stranger in Felicity Grove, someone I could confide in. Anna found too much mystique in mystery. Broghin had his own agenda. Wallace played it safe, expecting the world to run itself without him. Lowell Tully put honor and loyalty before most other principles, possibly even before justice. The rest of the town got their jollies from making up stories about Anubis mauling dead bodies. I had to position myself to be the balance, and I wasn't sure how to do it.

Katie materialized beside me like the phantom of the opera and said, "Hi there!"

I jumped and rapped my head on the Jeep's roll bar. "Jesus, don't do that."

She laughed pleasantly. "I thought it was you, Jonathan. I've been standing on the corner over there for five minutes. Nobody's ever been here before me, and I guess I got a little paranoid until I remembered you were driving a Jeep. You here for your tulips this early? You must have had a hell of a fight with your girlfriend. How long you been waiting?"

"Not very." I opened the door and she got her first real look at the swelling and bruises.

"Oh God, what have you been into?" Her eyes widened. "Your face. Did you at least get a few good licks in?" She touched my chin and yanked my head to one side so she could inspect the damage, like a mother about to spit-clean her son's cheeks before church.

"Yeah," I said. "Adonis envies me. Be careful where you're touching when lust consumes you and you're forced to smother me with kisses."

"But what happened?"

"Adonis was so jealous he beat the crap out of me."

"Hey." Her expression swung from alarm

to annoyance, pretty features shifting as she scowled at me. "Stop being a wiseass for a minute, will you please?"

"Somebody hit me repeatedly."

"Why?"

"No reason. You walk here from Margaret's house? That's where you're staying? It's got to be more than a mile away."

Katie gave an exasperated sigh. "You're not especially subtle when you switch the topic. You should work on that."

"So I've been told," I said.

"But to answer your question, no, I don't live there. I couldn't stay in her house knowing she'd died there. I took a cottage at The Orchard Inn complex, over on Prairie Lane. You know it? I was planning to get out and find my own apartment soon, but the rent is cheap and the place is so nice I don't see any rush. Come inside. You have coffee yet?"

"No," I said. My stomach still rumbled from the beer and tension last night. I rarely drank coffee, but could use a boost from caffeine. "I'd enjoy a cup."

"Decaf, okay?"

Damn it. "Fine."

She ushered me into the shop, flicking on lights as we entered. She had a graceful style to every movement, stepping with a ballerina's bounce. "Pardon me for a minute," she said, heading to the back room. I took off my coat and tossed it on a chair. Katie returned a minute later and filled the coffee maker with grounds and water, flipped through a number of papers stuck on a clipboard, checked the answering machine and had no messages. She plucked the phone receiver up and punched in a number. "This really can't wait. I've got to call these orders in or I'll be screwed up for another week. I never knew there were so many middle men and distributors and delivery services involved to these tiny stores. Pain in the ass."

I watched her talking fervidly to a guy named Carl, and it was time I considered well spent. Katie was mobile even on the phone, always in motion, fumbling the receiver into the crook of her neck as she grabbed two mugs off the shelf behind her. She wore a light beige blouse with a thin black belt and dark matching slacks, and her hair fell across her shoulder in such a way that — if I'd been more of a poet rather than a maker of stupid lists — I would have described as *cascading*. It fit her, the fluidity of the word. Her jade eyes flashed with thought while she talked, as readable as pages of a novel: piquancy, humor, interest, impatience. Apparently Carl didn't have enough of the flora she wanted, and he'd already sent on a number of items she didn't need.

Her expressive eyes were perplexed, forehead crinkling and smoothing as she searched through the papers on the clipboard and fiddled with the pencil attached to the clip by a string. "But I already have enough irises, Carl! Okay, okay . . . no, forget that, I'll mail the check on Thursday, and you'd better get me those yellow roses. No more red or whites or pinks. Yellow. Okay, are we clear on this now? Fine. Yellow. Goodbye, Carl." She hung up with a slam and said, "Jerk."

"The high pressure world of floral arrangements?"

"You'd be surprised. I'd think he was stabbing me in the back just to unload excess quantities of merchandise if I wasn't so sure he's too dim-witted. Do you think many people will want to buy azaleas and irises this month?"

"I only hope there won't be a rush on red, white, and pink roses."

"Me too." She turned and grinned her crooked grin, and my breath hitched in the same way it had when I'd first seen her. "By the way, your tulips came in late yesterday. They were already on back order so I didn't have to fill out an extra batch of forms. I don't know much about the actual process of growing flowers, what to do with the bulbs and seeds and the like, but I learned that tulips are out of season now. They'll start coming in for Easter. It was really just dumb luck that the first shipment arrived this week."

"Thanks for getting them. I appreciate the effort."

"Hey, it's my job to fulfill your floral needs." She put down the clipboard and pulled the chair with my coat on it beside her own behind the counter. "Jeez, I'm sorry, I haven't even asked you to sit down yet. Come on, don't wait for me." The coffee was ready and we sat and drank, and I watched her watching me, wondering if what was going through her head was anything like what was going through mine. I seriously doubted it.

Katie brushed her hair back off her shoulder. "Now, do you want to skip the humdrum pleasantries and get down to business and explain what happened to you?" She asked, voice an odd mixture of timidity and firmness. "Or shall we chat about the weather, Jon?"

"It's cold."

"Uh huh."

I chuckled, but it wasn't easy to open up; though I'd felt the need to speak with her about — I don't even know what about, just . . . *just* — I found it difficult deciding where to begin. If I told her about the bar and the fight, she wouldn't understand the reasoning unless I went back to the four AM call from Anna, and would *that* make sense unless I went further back to Jackson Whuller's murder five summers ago, and the baby-napper, and Phillip Dendren and the death of my parents? And maybe even that wasn't the beginning. I couldn't be sure. There were more disassembled pieces than I'd realized.

I wound up talking about my Mom and Dad, Michelle's tattoos and her leather-clad men, divorce and the bookstore and Debi and Gunter Grass, skipped to Richie Harraday in the trash and told it straight from there. She stopped me and asked questions to make sure she followed along; she wondered about mine and Lowell's friendship, and exactly what the beef with Broghin was. When I got to the part where I played freeze tag with the Dobermans, Katie sucked air and said, "I hate those dogs. There's something fundamentally insane with them."

For nearly an hour I continued, letting

most of it out while she listened, engrossed, occasionally quitting her seat to take care of a stray customer or three. She was friendly and courteous and had a knack for dealing with strangers. One of the things I liked most about Katie was her generosity with laughter. She was always ready to smile.

I brought the story up to the moment of sitting with her and feeling more relaxed than I had in three days. She asked why I hadn't called the police to have them search for the guy with the crew cut.

I told her, "The lady bartender said she'd call the cops. The doctor at the hospital filled out a report, and I'll talk to Lowell this afternoon. If the guy has a reputation for being a troublemaker anywhere in the five counties, Lowell will find him."

Katie changed position, lifted a leg and braced her heel on the chair, wrapped her arms around her knee. "You sound as if you respect him a great deal."

"I do. He saved my life once."

Obviously she wanted to hear more about that and my grandmother's current "case," but it must've been equally obvious that I didn't want to continue in that particular vein. She didn't press. I admired anyone with the strength to curb curiosity, a talent I didn't have.

Katie spoke for a while about herself, describing her past with broad strokes; an Army brat before her family settled in San Diego, writing music was a hobby, and she was one of the few people who actually liked those paintings of cigar-chomping dogs. "Ta da," she said when she'd finished.

We were silent then for several minutes; I wanted to know about her too, but now wasn't the time to ask more personal questions, so soon after my own discourse. She was one of the few women I've known who I felt comfortable with in silence. No need to fill the empty space because it really wasn't empty.

10:45. Katie stirred and maneuvered closer to me, brushing my pant leg, face ridiculously near mine while she poured herself another cup of coffee. "Would you like more?" she asked, and I waved off. Probably the perfect time to lean forward and kiss her, but I've been gun shy about first kisses since I'd stuck my lips out like a guppy for a woman who merely wanted to get close enough to gaze into my eyes because she'd been receiving obscene phone calls from a guy claiming his were "the color of saffron." My brown eyes either passed or failed, depending on your viewpoint, and she snapped her mouth away at the last second, leaving me sucking wind.

It wouldn't be that way with Katie, but at the moment my face was a bit too much like raw hamburger.

"Why did you decide to take over this shop?" I asked. "You were gearing up for a career in medicine and this seems a complete one-eighty."

"It's a reversal of sorts, that's for certain," she said. "You're probably waiting for me to tell you about seeing too much horror in the wards, viscera and pain and disease and all that, until my will was broken by staring into a terminally ill child's eyes, losing my faith in the world. Nothing so melodramatic as that. The truth is much simpler and a lot less entertaining. I could make the grades but I wasn't sure if I could make the cut."

"I'm not sure I know what that means."

"If I'd stuck to my guns I could've finished well in my class and gone on to a residency, but I don't think I would've made an especially good doctor. Or even a nurse. The pressures were enormous if you want to do it right. The ranks kept thinning every semester. There's a lot more to the medical profession than learning the parts of the body and writing prescriptions in an illegible scrawl. I didn't enjoy the baggage and finally gave it up before I wasted more of my time and tuition money."

"Is this what you want to do?"

"For the present. I like running this shop more than I thought I would. I enjoy helping the men pick out the right assortment for their wives or girlfriends." I told her about Margaret letting me skimp on my prom date's corsage and she nodded. "That was her, all right. On my sweet sixteen you should have seen the arrangement she had flown out to me. It took up the whole dining room table, and the house smelled like Eden for a week."

"Glad you're staying for a while."

She glanced out the window. "I can't get over this town. The entire first week I couldn't get my foot in the door without shoveling. Now, it's like Spring outside." She caught herself. "Seems I'm talking about the weather anyway."

"It's cold," I repeated.

"Uh huh."

"It's because of the Canadian winds flowing off Lake Ontario. When they come on strong they play havoc with the system and turn rain into snow, and snow into blizzards. It's the Lake Effect. When there's no wind, like today, you can finally feel the sunshine, the temperature the way it should be."

"Thank God. I'm not used to this kind of freeze. I'm missing the beaches badly. I haven't lost much of my tan yet, though, with the sunlight reflecting off the snow."

"Would you like to go out to dinner tomorrow night?" I asked.

"Sure," Katie said, smiling, jade eyes alive with sensitivity. "Just tell me one thing, Jonathan. Who are the tulips for again?"

Usually, because of the high winds up on the slopes, flowers didn't last long in the cemetery. Petals were stripped and Crummler immediately did his duty and cleaned the remains. Once I watched a plastic bouquet get kicked from grave to grave for about half an hour, wire prongs sticking for a while before flipping end over end to the next plot, as if spirits passed sentiment along. Crummler eventually chased it down and replaced the bouquet where it had originally been intended. He knew the spot, and he cared.

I put the tulips in front of the tombstones of my parents.

After six years, I had not completely gotten used to the fact they were gone. I thought I had cleared up all unfinished business when I'd found their killer, but now I understood that a part of me would never be at rest. Maybe, in some fashion it's better that way.

Phillip Dendren was my father's best friend and business partner in real estate for two decades. He'd taught me how to ride a bike and drive a car, and there were times I told him things I could never reveal or express to my Dad. He was there for me and my mother when the bottle got such a grip on my father that I could hardly recognize him anymore.

But long after my Dad had sobered and fought back his demons, a passing interest in gambling took a tighter hold on Uncle Phil. From what I later learned, he ran up exorbitant debts and dug a well for himself too deep to climb from. He never asked to borrow money from my father, who not only would have lent it to him, but being a reformed alcoholic also would have understood the consumptive nature of addiction. Perhaps Phil was more ashamed to face my Dad than he was to kill him.

After Anna roused from her coma and convinced Broghin to go searching three weeks late for a murderer in a gray Caddy, I began the hunt for the killer myself. The police went to work looking for a crazed driver, and coincidence gave Broghin's theory some credence: two counties to the east, in the mill town of Walkerwood, there had recently been a similar type of thrill-killing. A black truck driver had been forced off the road, robbed, and beaten to death with a flashlight. Broghin sought a connection.

I've tried to imagine what I would have thought and felt if the police had captured Phillip Dendren instead of my confronting him that night at Jackals. I'm certain I would have found at least a passing moment of sympathy, or more appropriately, pity, but I could never forgive the pure premeditated nature of his actions. They weren't those of a man enslaved, but rather of someone who coming into his own, discovering how much he enjoyed the foulness of his own weak nature.

Not only was Phillip Dendren my father's business partner and friend, but he was also my Dad's attorney. Six months before he ran my parents' car off the Turnpike, my father had gone to him to have his will slightly amended because I'd just turned twenty-one; perhaps that had inspired Dendren to murder.

My father trusted him implicitly and wouldn't have bothered to read before signing; Dendren realized this and made his own additions, bestowing nearly the whole of the business to him in the event of my father's death. He was smart and slick and more imaginative than I would've given him credit for, because he made it look perfect in the paperwork, as if my Dad gave everything to Dendren so that he could watch over my mother and me. How sweet. And because Anna was in a coma and I was in jail for throwing a chair at the sheriff, Dendren had the two of us sewn up away from the action so that we couldn't question the execution of my parents' estate. By the time we were released from our respective prisons, neither cared enough to bother with the legalities. He'd wrapped the package nice and tight with a big, bright bow.

Even now it tears hell out of my guts when I think too hard about the ease with which my Uncle Phil had reached down and wrung my mother's neck.

Suspicion was further thrown off him by the fact that he was very nearly the victim of a hit and run himself — by a car driven by the men he owed a cool quarter million. So that it actually appeared as if there was a psychotic driver on the loose. Gunning for anyone, and everyone.

But Dendren made his mistakes; little things mostly, but they helped trip him up. Like lying about why he didn't visit me in jail, claiming he was busy taking care of business, and then my discovering he hadn't been seen in town for weeks and had asked another associate to wire him money in New Jersey. On a couple of occasions I noticed slight stains on his shoes and grease under his nails. A page on his desk filled with numbers and equations that made no sense. They were just nosy questions I had, little hints here and there. Nothing, in the long and short run, but it went into the recesses of my subconscious.

After a month of staking out Walkerwood I'd stumbled onto the flashlight killer, who'd already murdered two more people; he was a deranged gas station attendant named Cuthbert who killed drivers by the quarter moon, and I'd been saved from him by Lowell's exceptional timing. In a mountain cabin retreat Cuthbert had tried to crown me and his own sister, and Lowell had been forced to shoot him dead.

Solved, so far as the police were concerned, but the anomalies, the differences between the deaths, stuck too far out for me. I admitted my suspicions to Uncle Phil, who always listened and supported me through the whole painful ordeal. Fearing I'd learn the truth soon, he invited me over for dinner and a movie and let me crap out on the couch. In the morning, after just about my only good night of rest in the four months since the death of my parents, I got into my car and started to drive home with disconnected brake lines.

I wound up sharing a private hospital room with Anna, six ribs cracked, a bruised Atlas vertebra, and more sprains than I could count, seeing my immobile grandmother in her casts and her agony and never complaining about what it was to now be paralyzed. Watching her, I thought about the horror following us; where the real murderer of my parents might hide a car, and wondering about other safe havens for another killer, and I remembered the abandoned garage in town on property owned by my father, now owned by Dendren. And the numbers and equations were percentages: systems to beat the odds, notes by a madman who'd been beaten by them. And thoughts turned more rapidly: casinos in Atlantic City, New Jersey, my father's money, the grease and rust stains on Uncle Phil's clothes, and the chance to cut my brakes.

Still half-sedated, running a fever, I hobbled out of bed against Anna's protests as the facts came together in a hazy red rush. I left the hospital and went to the garage and discovered the caddy. I remember screaming and weeping, and I searched and finally found him at Jackals. We stared into each other's eyes until his smile melted into a greasy sneer and he realized that I knew; there was no remorse in that gaze as he pulled a .32 from an ankle holster and shot me, and my momentum and rage carried me forward onto him, and the gun went off again over my left shoulder and I beat his brains out against the bar railing.

"Christ," I whispered.

My attention suddenly snapped from their graves to the shack. Zebediah Crummler waved in the distance, jogging towards me. "I am here, Jon!" he called cheerfully. He stood trembling and jitterbugging on the balls of his feet, toes of his new workboots pointing. "I keep them clean. I have not stepped in mud."

"I wish I could say the same."

He laughed and patted me on the back and scratched his wild beard. "Forces from the dark domain throw their evil upon our world. I must fight them for I am Crummler! And the universal battle between chaos and order is never ending. Stars have been born and died in the same breath while . . ." He kept going, bopping and weaving between frenzy and exhilaration, but I didn't listen anymore. The occasional

"Uh huhs" and "yeahs" I muttered were enough to keep him happy.

"Your folks are nice," he said.

"Yes, they are."

"The ghost was here again," he said. "Chasing me with the willow swatches."

"What did you do to him?"

Crummler slunked low where he stood, grin gone. "I ran and locked the door and read the Bible." His eyes flitted, intense features contorting from his usual amiable countenance into someone who was panic-stricken. "It banged on the windows and said that it hated me."

No matter what weird fantasies and stories he came up with, Crummler was always vibrant and filled with manic passion. Now he stood before me a scared child. "Why?"

"It wouldn't tell me, but I think it's mad because I didn't keep its grave nice."

"You keep all the graves nice. You keep the cemetery immaculate."

"Yes, I do," he answered. "But not the Field."

Every town has a Potter's Field, whether they admit to it or not. Felicity Grove's was at the southern tip of the cemetery, an overgrown area straight out of a gothic novel. The twisted brushline strangled itself, branches growing together locked in battle.

Even Crummler couldn't do much with the landscape, though he tried. But he didn't like to cut down trees, even those dead and diseased, and so the place was destined to decay because too many people before him had let the field become dense and rotted.

"Show me," I said.

He led me to the place where the vagrants, aborted, mad and the hanged were buried nearly a century before. These were un-marked graves, identified only by a number carved into stone near the bottom.

There were willow swatches laid against the marker.

"Who is buried here?"

"Nobody," he answered.

"There must still be records."

"They're nobody," he said. "They are all nobody." He pointed. "Unholy ground. It's where they used to put the criminals and abandoned babies they found. Pauper's funeral. The county pays. Now they give them real gravestones on the other side of the yard."

"What's the most recent plot here in the Field?"

"It was a long time ago, but I remember. Ten years, maybe. Or eleven. I wasn't that good at taking care of the place back then."

That wasn't so long ago, I thought. Even

so recent as ten years ago our town was burying its lost dead here without so much as a name.

"It's better to let them stay buried, Jon," Crummler said. "Nobodies don't like to be moved around much." He shuddered and snapped his fingers, the wire burning again. He smiled brightly. "I sure didn't."

8

Church bells pealed twelve, resonating sadly across the town square. Instead of being vitalized by the gorgeous afternoon, the lack of sleep was catching up with me, and I found myself sluggish and grim. My stitches were on fire. The time I'd spent with Katie had been overshadowed by memories of murder, and for the first time since my childhood, Crummler's rantings disturbed me. And I didn't know why.

My stomach had been rumbling for a while before I noticed hunger pangs had set in. I stopped at the Maple Ridge Diner to get some lunch. The waitress came around to take my order and I let out a loud, raspy yawn. "Sorry. I don't mean to be rude."

"That's okay, I know how you feel," she said. "Two girls are out sick and I've been here since the six AM rush. I'm ready for a siesta myself." She had a copy of today's *Gazette* under her arm. "In case you want to read something. Most guys do when they're eating alone." Apparently Merlin's turkey was no longer noteworthy news. The head-

133

line read: FALLEN TREE DAMAGES COUNTY CLERK'S DOGHOUSE. NO ONE HURT. *"Good thing Chase was inside for the night!"* says owner, Mitchell Luserke.

I asked for a turkey on rye and tossed the paper aside. She brought the sandwich in five minutes. After eating, I felt much more awake and decided to stop in and see Lowell. I needed to tell him about the fight, which he had probably heard about already, but more importantly I wanted to know if he'd discovered anything about Broghin and the note possibly left on Richie Harraday's corpse. And I still had to find out about Tons.

There was a minor car accident at the crossroads of Monroe and Stonewall Avenues, and traffic had snarled ridiculously in the vicinity: I got the feeling that people enjoyed being involved in grid-lock, it was something new to do. I had enough room to back up and turn around in a gas station and circumvent the area but nobody else followed my lead. I pulled in to the police station and saw Lowell's cruiser parked out front.

The central heating control to the building must've been stuck at full tilt. As I walked in the blast of hot air was enough to sway me in my tracks. Half a dozen deputies milled the station, guys with their sleeves rolled up and shirts unbuttoned to their navels while the two lady officers simply wore tank-tops and pony-tails. Heat must've been broken all winter. I checked the sheriff's office and saw he wasn't in.

Lowell's door was ajar, and he sat with his feet up on his desk. He stared intently out an open window, and the set of his jaw was enough to get the hair on my nape prickling. I barely caught his eye before he swung out of the chair and said, "Let's go, Johnny."

Sweat had already formed on my upper lip, and it was difficult to breathe with the heat so high. "Cripes yes, before we broil like steaks. Do we have a destination in mind this time?"

"Aren't you going to mention how I look like hell?"

"Hell's a little high on the ladder," Lowell said. "You know Freeman Hofferball got a farm out in West Stokes?"

"Handsome fellow."

"Had himself a prize sow called Gertie broke all kinds of local records?"

"Beautiful pig."

"Slaughtered Gertie and sold the pork to Fred Mudrell owns the Maple Ridge Diner?"

"Fred's a lovely guy."

"I went in and ordered myself a lunch special of ham, string beans and sweet potatoes — Fred's got himself a wonderful cook knows how to do the sweet potatoes just right — and the waitress brought it out to me?"

"Cute chick."

"And she dropped it halfway across the room and accidentally stepped on it? At the moment your face is more on par with *that,* I'd have to say."

"I'm a fellow who can take a compliment," I told him. "In case you were wondering."

"C'mon."

In the car I asked, "You been waiting for me?"

He ignored the question. "Who've you been tangling with?"

"Guy with a crew cut, swimmer's body, and a bad disposition. Crazy calm eyes, the kind that can spook you. He was at Raimi's last night, drunk and needling me into a fight."

"And you obliged him."

"It wasn't my choice, Lowell," I said.

"No, he just happened to pick a tussle with you out of everybody in a crowded bar."

"I didn't go looking for it."

"I'm sure you did your damndest to persuade him differently. It's not like you to make an asshole with a mad-on blow his goddamn lid."

"I didn't offer him an olive branch if that's what you're after. You would have?"

"Nope," he said.

"Then there we are."

We drove a similar route to the one we had the other day, meandering around the high school, the lumber yard, and the movie theater where the latest Schwarzenegger flick was playing. I didn't feel like listening to Lowell get self-righteous about my poor diplomatic relations with jackasses looking to carve me up, especially when I'd seen him break as many arms as I had. He made Schwarzenegger look like Albert Schweitzer.

"Look," I said as we doubled back towards the power station. "It's a nice view, but I've seen it before. What'd you find out about Broghin?"

Lowell wore his agitation on his sleeve, and from the way he kept his chin down to his chest I could see he was clearly ashamed of himself for something. With the way everybody was acting lately, I'd slipped far past being spooked and entered new realms of jumpiness. The cords in his neck stood out like steel cables. He frowned and let out a stream of breath that fogged the inside of the windshield. "It was an old love letter from his wife, for Christ's sake. Reading it made me feel like a pervert going through Clarice's underwear drawer."

"A love letter?" I repeated. Of all the possibilities I'd turned back and forth in my mind, that one came from way out in left field. "You sure?"

"What in the hell kind of question is that? Of course, I'm sure. Darling, I can't wait to make love to you again. You make my heart sing. That kind of stuff. I can't believe I let you talk me —"

I cut him off; his cop instincts were conflicting with his loyalties, and I proved the easiest target to foist blame on. I wasn't in the mood. "I didn't talk you into anything. You were the one who said you thought Richie's killer left a note, that something wasn't clicking on the night of the murder and the note made a connection."

His voice went smooth and quiet. "Well, I was wrong."

"You don't really believe that." A crust of falling snow came down on top of the cruiser as we drove under Chapel Bridge. "Did you read the whole thing?"

"Enough of it."

"What the hell does that mean, Lowell?"

"It's nothing for you and me to be concerned about. I was wrong."

"Even about Broghin being rattled?"

He paused. He didn't like me playing devil's advocate, but the reason he'd been waiting for me today was so I could do exactly that. Where this went was more a battle of wills than a matter of facts. Would my and Anna's pushy imaginations win out over the cut-and-dried police investigation? I'd been in Felicity Grove for three days and nothing had happened so far concerning the murder — if it was a murder. Richie's body being left on my grandmother's lawn appeared more like coincidence every day, and if that were true, I could leave for Manhattan anytime. Just so long as I could be sure she was safe.

"You were certain Broghin was on edge because he was hiding something," I said. "You thought he or his family had been threatened."

Lowell sternly faced ahead, stopping at a stop sign and waving a woman and her two children across. "He must be having troubles with Clarice. They get into their moods, and they've both got rotten tempers. I've seen them go at it a couple of times before. Afterwards, she cooks him his favorite dinner and he buys flowers and they're as cuddly as a couple of panda bears."

"Lowell, I know you're feeling divided right now but you should have read the whole note. That was sloppy, and you're not sloppy. Why would Broghin be sitting in his office rereading an old love letter from his wife?"

"He probably dug it up to remind himself of when things were better. Men do strange things when they're fighting with their wives."

"And their consciences," I said. "You know you're going to come around soon enough, so stop arguing."

His knuckles went white on the steering wheel and I thought: If he hits me in the center of my forehead I won't even look as good as a plateful of ham on the floor.

"What about the dry spot on Richie's leg?" I asked.

He shrugged his massive shoulders. "I don't know," he said half-heartedly. "I may have been mistaken."

"You're fighting yourself at every turn here, Lowell. This involves Broghin in some stupid way and you don't want to believe it. All right, I have a bias against the man and don't really think he's all that big a fool, but something's going on here. It's probably something dumb or macho, but it's getting in his way. He's your boss, friend and mentor, I suppose, and you've seen him put his life on the line. That means a lot. That loyalty of yours proves you're a hell of a man, but maybe it's too thick for you to see the truth."

"Which is?"

"We still have to find out. And we aren't going to do it by playing blind civil servant."

His chin snapped up. "Christ. You're still one for talking big when you haven't got much to say, Johnny."

"Is it possible that this love letter *had* been left on the body?"

We came to a red light and he turned and stared at me. I felt like I had when we'd been in high school and losing to a better team and there was time for one last play, maybe, with a chance to tie, not even to win but just to tie, and we'd look at each other across the huddle knowing we had only a thread to hang on to, hardly recognizable with the mud and grease paint, both of us feeling the weight of ephemeral glory on our backs along with the momentary hopes of our girl-friends and families and the rest of the fans in the stands, wondering if we'd blow it. "How should I know?" he said. "Anything is possible."

"Then we —"

The dispatcher came over his radio in a sharply garbled crackle: "Lowell?"

He snatched the transceiver. "I'm here, Meg."

I could barely make out her words. Meg spoke rapidly, the static blaring: "Jackie Bubrick just called. Says her daughter and no good son-in-law are going at it again, and this time Aaron's hopped into it, too. Getting ugly. Somebody's waving a gun around."

"Who is it, Meg?"

"She was wailing and didn't say. Maybe Aaron decided to clean house all by himself."

"I'm only three miles away."

"You want I should send another car?"

"No, I'll handle it," he said and slung the transceiver.

He stomped the gas pedal but didn't put on his lights or siren. "Third time I've been here in as many weeks." We slipped through the back roads, and he made a few quick rights and sped down a winding street for several blocks to a dead end where the snow plows hadn't done a good job. The cruiser slid in slush and Lowell pulled up at a dingy house, wheeling into a long driveway and parked at a cool cop car angle. Once he cut the engine we could hear distant yelling inside. The storm door hung askew from one hinge as if somebody had either barged in or rushed out.

"Do you want me to stay in the car?" I asked.

"Do what you want," Lowell said.

I wasn't sure what to make of his reply so I followed him up the porch. Lowell had to yank the storm door aside to get in. The top hinge snapped as he entered, and the door practically fell into my arms. Lowell walked in and said, "Sheriff's department," in a booming, authoritative voice. I thought I was right behind him, but by the time I got the door propped against the siding he was gone.

From somewhere deep in the house, a girl yelled, "Don't! Daddy, no!" Another woman, Jackie Bubrick I presumed, continued to wail. I peered into a dining room full of overturned chairs, shattered dishes, and the remains of meatloaf on the floor. There was a crash. I followed the sounds down a corridor which led to basement stairs. Lowell stood at the bottom with his arms crossed across his chest, and I walked down to stand beside him.

The basement had actually been a small furnished apartment, and was now the fragments of one. The brawl that apparently started upstairs during lunch had been taken down here. A busted 12" television lay keeled over in the midst of other scattered bric-a-brac, wisps of gray smoke trailing from the broken screen.

A sobbing girl of about twenty, dressed in jeans and a cotton blouse, cried in the far corner, holding a chipped vase close to her chest. Her stomach was slightly distended; she was at least five months pregnant. Dried blood speckled her nostrils and there was an ugly purple welt along her neck. She was being hugged by her mother, a large woman wearing a pink housecoat, sobbing hysterically and with so much hair piled into a tight bun at the top of her head that it looked like a pin prick would explode her head.

Two men were in the center of the room among the wreckage of a stereo system and broken tables. Aaron Bubrick was fiftyish, his hair in a tangle, clothes rumpled and collar ripped. He breathed heavily and leaned back against a wall. His son-in-law was sprawled on the floor on his hands and knees; the kid was in sweatpants and a gravy-stained T-shirt. He looked younger than the girl, acne-ridden face twisted into a road map of rage, staring over his shoulder at Aaron. Both men had gashes on their arms and were bleeding from their mouths.

The kid had tears of fury dribbling from his eyes and there was spittle on his chin. Aaron Bubrick had a .38 automatic pointed at the head of his daughter's husband.

"Daddy, let him up!" she shouted.

Jackie Bubrick wept and held her tighter. She choked out, "Aaron, you damn fool. Put that pistol away before you hurt somebody."

"Don't, Daddy! Please, it's okay now!"

Aaron Bubrick gave them both curt nods and rubbed the back of his hand across his smeared cheeks. "Don't what, Angie? Ten minutes ago you were shrieking like a banshee, screaming you hated his guts and wished him dead and wanted me to make him leave you alone."

Wild alarm and guilt filled Angie's eyes. "But he . . . he's learned his lesson."

"I'm not inclined to agree with you, Angie."

"Tell him, Dean!"

"There's nothing he can tell me."

"Tell him, Dean! Tell him you won't —"

From the floor, Dean muttered, "Shut up, you bitch." He seemed to want to murder everyone in the room and then go out and club baby seals.

With his free hand balled into a fist, Aaron punched the boy solidly between the shoulder blades and pushed him down hard.

"I'd say you're all for proving my point, boy."

"When I get up, old man, I'm —"

"You'll do nothing unamiable less you want a hole in your chest, that's for sure."

"I'm gonna —"

"You'll pack your bags and get out of my house, you stinking parasite!" Up until then, Aaron had a hold on his anger, but his neck flushed and those strange alien veins men in their fifties get at their temples suddenly pulsed. "You've been sponging off me for a year now, and never a word of thanks in all that time. You're one of the worst chiselers I've ever seen. An able-bodied man like you sleeping 'til noon and not bothering to go looking for a job. Not even caring. And with a child on the way." He shook his head in disbelief. "And then you slap her for no reason. My daughter. A pregnant girl."

Dean's lips crawled into a sneer. "She's got your big mouth."

"Get up and get out, boy."

Lowell moved for the first time since we'd come in on the scene. His walk was slow and his motions non-threatening. He kept his arms crossed, I thought, so that no one would mistake him for going for his gun.

"You about done, Aaron?" he asked.

"Soon as this piece of shit runt gets his

scrawny tail out of my house."

"I'll go," Dean murmured. "Let me just tell my wife how much —"

"No, I don't think so," said Aaron. "You can call her from a Motel Six."

From my angle on the stairs I had a better view of what was about to happen than either Lowell or Aaron Bubrick. I saw Dean's shoulder muscles bunch and his thighs knot up; he sprang forward. No chance to call out. Aaron dropped his arm a few inches so the boy could rise and Dean wheeled and hit him in the forearm. Lowell moved at almost the same moment. Dean was closer and shoved Aaron aside and wrestled the gun from his numb hand. The struggle lasted only an instant but the barrel had been pointed directly at my feet during that time. An image of my footless body toppling down the steps lit my head. Aaron cried out and fell backwards as Dean kneed him in the groin, holding the .38 now. Once Lowell realized he was not going to beat Dean to the gun, he quickly stepped in front of Aaron. The older man doubled over, gasping and trying to catch his breath. I didn't know what to do so I didn't do anything.

Dean's bloody smile was like a scrape across his face, teeth showing red. He wasn't sure who to take his anger out on, his father-in-law or the deputy, his wife or her mother. He looked around from one to another, and his gaze thankfully passed over me as if I were invisible. Lowell Tully's barrel chest blocked him from getting a bead on Aaron, so finally Dean settled for pointing the gun at Lowell.

"You didn't even pull him off me!" he shouted.

"Nope," Lowell said.

"He was gonna kill me!"

"Seems to me you were getting a little taste of what you give."

"You son of a bitch."

Lowell's granite features never altered. His eyes had a scary glaze like a wolverine's, blazing with intensity, and he looked that much more deadly because he acted so passively. "Dean, if you put that gun down in the next five seconds you might be able to walk out of here on your own. Otherwise you're going to the hospital. And then to jail for a lot longer than you'll be able to handle."

Dean brought the .38 up and held it pointed directly between Lowell's eyes. The pit of my stomach did flip-flops and my groin tightened. If he pulled the trigger I'd have to kill the kid.

"You like being in control," Lowell said to him, as if discussing a good book. "Noticed that about you from the first. It's why you like being married to Angie, 'cause you figure you can always be in charge, slap her around now and then, put her in her place."

"You don't know anything. You don't know a goddamn thing about me."

Lowell nodded to himself. "It's why you hate living under the same roof as her parents. 'Cause you can't get away with everything all the time. They get on your back. But you're too lazy to get a job and earn your own way, so it's a wash. Builds the pressure up inside, don't it?"

"I don't need a lecture from you!" Dean shouted.

"You need to listen to somebody, kid. Your free ride is over, and you're making matters worse. You think you got power in your hand right now, but all you've got is more trouble than you've ever had in your miserable life. You couldn't pull the trigger if I paid you."

"Don't be too sure."

"That's the one thing I've been sure about all day."

"Don't dare me," Dean said. "I've used a gun before, plenty of times. My father knew everything about them and he taught me. You're standing there and you're talking at me and daring me. Don't do that."

I agreed with him. I didn't understand how Lowell could continue to speak so calmly when he was literally staring down the barrel of a gun; I also thought it was excessively stupid for him to piss off a crazy kid who might pull the trigger accidentally just as soon as aim to blow somebody's brains out.

"Put it down," Lowell said.

"Do it, Dean," Angie pleaded. "Please. Everything will be okay, I promise."

The confusion played in his glare. "You always do that, Angie! You always make promises you can't keep." He didn't want to let go of what little power he had in the world and return to being a boy with no job and a pregnant wife and to live beneath the roof of a man who rightfully talked down to him. "Oh, shit." The blood drained from the kid's face until he was just another nineteen-year-old standing there without any edge on the future. Angie dumped the chipped vase and broke from her mother's grasp. She rushed to him, and the two of them hugged and she started to cry against his chest and he looked around the room searching for answers that nobody had.

Two more deputies clattered at the top of the stairs, came down and pressed past me and looked at the scene without any surprise.

Lowell said to them, "I told Meg I had everything under control."

"I know," one of the other deputies answered. "But that place was just too damn hot."

Driving back to the station, Lowell said, "Told you men do strange things when they're fighting with their wives."

"And their consciences."

He grunted. "Yeah."

Icy fingers still kneaded my back. "You wanted me to see you in action. To get back at me for making that crack about civil servants."

"What crack?" he asked.

"Oh boy."

The entire episode hardly affected him. "You ever think about when we were kids?"

"Stick to the subject."

"Do you?"

"I've been doing nothing else lately."

"Me, too. Why do you think that is?"

I thought about it and couldn't come up with an adequate answer. "Mid-life crisis?"

"At twenty-nine?" He laughed for the first time all afternoon. "I hope to Christ not. That doesn't say a hell of a lot for our longevity."

9

I hated the thought of dealing with the Dobermans again, but I wanted to find out why Tons Harraday hadn't shown at the bar last night. I got lost again driving up the back hills and wound up passing the same gas station as before. I turned around and went east of Warner fork and made it to his place without any more trouble.

This time I didn't park at the bottom of the driveway. I checked for the dogs, didn't see them, and drove straight up across the snowy lawn to the foot of the front door. I hopped out of the Jeep and rushed for the small and rotted, sagging porch. Still no sign of the Dobermans. Tons' motorcycle sat at the side of the house near the trailer.

I knocked on the metal frame of the storm door and waited, trying hard not to keep checking over my shoulder. A half minute passed and I knocked again, much louder. A deadbolt snicked back, the lock clacked, and the front door opened with a huff of air.

Tons' wife, Deena, stood looking at me without a hint of expression. Her unnaturally scarlet hair was splayed around her neck and shoulders, down to the waist, much longer than I'd originally thought. She proved to be prettier, too, than I remembered. Her nose didn't seem so long or mouth so crooked, and her breasts arched lissomely against the silky blouse; she possessed that unnamable sensual quality certain women have, and it was like having a powerful charge snapping at me to be so near it.

Deena continued to stare impassively, eyes so emotionless that she appeared blind, and didn't say anything. Fred and Barney watched me from around her skirt with their cute names and their cute uncut ears and their equally deadpan eyes. Some days you just can't plan well enough. This house must be a ball at Christmas.

She pushed open the storm door and said, "Yes?"

"I'm looking for your husband," I said.

"He's asleep."

I checked my watch. "At four in the afternoon?" The dogs nudged a step closer, and I wished she'd let them out and let me slip in. "Could you wake him please?"

She smiled without humor. "You'd think that was a normal request, but you don't know what you're asking. I don't need to hear his yelling and bitching."

"It's important," I said.

"Who are you?" she asked.

"My name's Jonathan Kendrick. I was here yesterday afternoon."

"I remember. I just didn't know your name."

"Tons was supposed to meet me last night at Raini's and never showed."

"What do you want to talk to him about?"

Tons had said he'd wanted to ask questions of me, too, and I wondered why. How much did Deena know about her brother-in-law Richie, and could she shed some light on what might have happened to him? Nobody seemed to know much about what he was into or who he might have been mixed up with — it suddenly struck me that I'd forgotten to ask Lowell if Margaret's jewelry had ever been found. Tons had said Richie was a quiet and shy kid who kept to himself; if that were true, Richie may have told things to Deena he wouldn't have spoken about to his own brother.

I said, "I'm just trying to find out a little more about Richie."

The muscles in her face softened all at once, leaving her with an even blanker expression if that was possible. "Richie was a good kid."

"Do you know if he was hanging around

with anyone in particular?"

She shook her head. "No."

"A close buddy? A girlfriend?"

Her voice grew faraway. "I already told you no. He had no friends or girlfriends at all that I know of. He stuck to himself. He never wanted any trouble."

"Why do you think he broke into Margaret Gallagher's house?" I asked.

Flakes of snow sprinkled off the rain gutters and landed at our feet, light breeze whirling them between her bare toes. She shivered and hugged herself, but didn't ask me in. "So he did stupid things every once in a while. He was just a kid. He never would have hurt anyone."

"I don't know. How long did you know him?"

"Since I met Tons, of course. A year and a half ago." The amount of time seemed to impress her, and those thread-thin eyebrows fluttered and a wrinkle creased her forehead. "Somehow it doesn't seem that long ago, and in another way it feels much longer."

"Did he ever mention why he —"

"Why do you keep asking so many questions?"

"Because his body was found virtually on my grandmother's doorstep, and I want to know if that means something."

"How could it mean anything?"

My next question was cut off by a loud, low groan from the back room.

"It's awake," Deena said.

Tons stumbled behind her into the kitchen, wearing only sagging boxer shorts and a black T-shirt with the sleeves sliced off that said HARLEY RULES. My ex-wife would have loved him. "Get me a glass of juice," he croaked. "Jesus, it's cold. Shut the damn door will you, baby." He fell over into a kitchen chair and the floor rocked.

"There's somebody here to see you," she told him.

He peered around her to look at me but the sunlight was enough to blind him. "Who?"

"Jonathan Kendrick," I said.

"*Who?*"

"Guess you should come in," Deena said.

The dogs backed off and went to Tons and he swatted them away, grousing. Fred and Barney sat in the center of the small, cluttered living room and looked at me the same way the information clerks at Motor Vehicles will look at you.

Empty beer cans littered the floor and a quarter bottle of Scotch peeked out between the cushions of the couch; Tons had spent the night drinking alone at home rather than at the bar.

"You again," he said.

"Me again," I said.

"What do you want now?"

"To find out why you never showed at Raimi's last night."

"Huh?" he said, peering at my face as if he occasionally recognized me but kept forgetting from second to second. "Oh yeah, shit. We were gonna talk." Deena brought him a tall glass of V-8. He slurped half the contents down in one pull, then pressed the cold glass against his forehead. He burped and said, "One of them nights."

"Yeah." It wasn't hard to see where Richie may have inherited his drug problem.

Tons drank the rest of the V-8 and Deena filled a second glass for him. He squinted so hard that his large face scrunched into strange, fleshy angles. "Somebody sure came down on you."

"Raimi's doesn't always draw a friendly crowd."

"Ain't that the truth."

"I was hoping we could finish our talk."

"What time is it?" He spotted a clock on the kitchen counter, reached over and pulled it to within six inches of his eyes. "Four o'clock?"

Deena moved behind him, cleaning dishes in the sink. "You slept in big time today."

"Oh, man." He pushed the clock away from him. "Baby, why didn't you stop me when you got home last night?"

"Like that's my responsibility? I've got to take care of an infant, work, and watch out for you, too? You're over eighteen, you do what you want."

"Why didn't you show up?" I said.

He sipped the juice. "I don't know. I meant to, but . . . I got to thinking, after our talk, about my brother, and I just started drinking some beer, and . . ." He let the sentence drift. "Maybe you can't understand this, but he's been dead four days now and it feels like I'm *just* noticing, you know? That make any sense?"

"Yes," I said.

"I sound like an ass."

"It's tough to put into words."

"Do you kinda feel like that, Deena?" he asked.

She nodded slowly. "Yeah."

Tons closed his eyes and rolled the glass over the bridge of his nose.

"You mind if I take a look around Richie's room?"

Deena gave me a puzzled glance. "Why?"

"I don't know."

"Cops were already here," Tons said. "They can try and pin whatever the hell they want on him, it ain't gonna do anybody any good now. What's the point?"

I nodded. "I'd still like to look around. If you don't mind."

He shrugged. "Who gives a damn? Go ahead."

"I'll show you," Deena said. "But be quiet. Kristine is sleeping." She led me past the dogs to the back of the house. The one large window faced the East so the room was relatively dark. Either someone had cleaned his bedroom or Richie Harraday had been an exceptionally neat kid. The top of the dresser had been kept well-polished. There was a rifle rack with two BB guns over the headboard. Directly on top of that was another rack with three fishing poles.

On the far wall rested a tack board covered with the usual: stickers, pennants, and group photographs. I realized I'd never seen a picture of Richie Harraday and asked Deena to point him out. She chose a family shot down by the river: Tons had a beer in one hand toasting the camera, his other arm thrown around Deena, who was smiling seductively, hair alive in the wind. I got another charge from her, seeing those bedroom eyes, and wondered how she'd wound up with a guy named, at his best, Tons, and at his worst, Maurice. Richie stood a couple of feet to one side of Deena, a noncommital smirk on his face. I didn't know what I'd expected, but he looked more average than I would have thought: wavy brown hair, round face like his brother, *Beverly Hills 90210* sideburns thick and well-trimmed. He was just a rather clean-cut looking kid, and if I had a baby sister I would've preferred that Richie took her out than the enraged, acne-riddled maniacal Dean.

Deena grinned sadly and pointed out a couple other photos of Richie. "This one was taken at the sheet metal factory where Tons works part-time."

"Did Richie work?"

"Nah, not really. He picked up a few bucks here and there, but nothing steady. He tried but never got his diploma. He would have graduated last year, but he had to take summer school and Richie wasn't the type to give up his summers for anything."

I didn't want to search Richie's room while Deena was present but she made it obvious she wasn't about to leave. I tossed the room anyway, starting in his closet. Nothing unusual, just clothes and ordinary hideaway junk. Drawers of his dresser were the same, as were the two shelves beside the tack board. Nothing struck me as odd until I opened his night stand. There was an open box of condoms.

"I think maybe he had a girlfriend after all," I said.

Deena frowned. "Hell, anybody can get laid. It only costs a couple bucks."

"Would a shy kid like Richie go to a pro?"

"I can't imagine it, really, but if he had a girlfriend he never brought her home or talked about her. Why wouldn't he have told me?"

"Was he gay?"

The narrow eyebrows moved liked spiders. "If Tons heard you ask that he'd beat you to your knees."

"That's not really an answer," I said.

"No, I don't think so. I'm not sure what Richie was, and this is starting to get a little rude for my tastes, if you know what I mean."

"Were you close?"

"I thought we were, but Richie was so quiet you just took it for granted that he had his secrets like everybody. He didn't talk enough about what was on his mind. He kept too much to himself." Her voice had consistently faded as she spoke, until now she was barely whispering. "His funeral's the day after tomorrow, if you want to come."

I looked at his photographs again — a nice-looking boy with a self-conscious smile, his eyes anything but shrewd — and thought, Jesus Christ, kid, how did you end up in my trash?

The roads were slick getting back, melting snow turning to ice as night fell. The sheen of black ice made for especially dangerous driving. I switched on the radio and the newscaster said our streak of one beautiful day was at an end, and we could expect six more inches of snow by morning.

I pulled into Anna's driveway, but decided I should speak with Jim Witherton at least once. I'd talked with everybody else I could think of and wanted to be thorough before I told Anna I'd been punched out, stitched in the emergency room, troubled by Crummler, involved in a family dispute and learned absolutely nothing all day. I jogged down to Jim's house. No light showed through his windows. I knocked, waited, tried again. Still no answer.

I walked back to Anna's and let myself in.

Anubis wandered over and stared stoically at me. I should've brought him to Harraday's house to kick the shit out of

Fred and Barney. He stepped forward and stuck his tongue out to lick my hand but didn't quite make it. He slurped his lips and turned and went back into the bedroom.

"Jonathan?" Anna called.

"It's me," I said. "I'll be there in a minute." I went to the refrigerator and wished I'd stocked up on beer. The hardest drink we had was milk, so I poured myself a double. I actually had a hankering for some cookies, but I wouldn't be caught dead having milk and cookies in my grandmother's house. Somebody might write me into a nursery rhyme.

Anna didn't want to wait. I heard her throw a book aside and wheel herself out into the kitchen.

"Where have you been?" she said, as close to angry as she usually gets. "Why haven't you called?'

"Anna."

I turned, and when she saw the bruises er face tightened. "You've been in a fight. When? With who? What have you been doing? Explain yourself."

I pulled a chair from the table and drank my milk and she sat next to me. Anubis kept he side of his head pressed to her leg and occasionally gurgled and moaned. I told her what had happened at Raimi's and she listened thoughtfully but tsked a lot; shudders of irritation run up my back whenever she tsks me.

"Are you in much pain?"

"No," I said.

"Did you pound him to within an inch of his life?"

"No, but I've got a much better hair style."

"Well," she sighed, "I suppose that is something."

It was odd, but — sitting there and sensing the sharp and keen presence of her strength — I felt especially weak in comparison, a failure by default. She held her finger up like a teacher making an important point about the atomic weight of Bromide. "You shouldn't be off all day probing this case on your own. You know as well as I do how dangerous that can be, and you wear the scars for it. I insist you inform me of your whereabouts and . . ."

"Anna, I'm not ten years old."

"Then I suggest you stop acting like a petulant child, always forcing me to reprimand you because you enjoy it so much. Do not approach this case with such obstinacy, Jonathan. The time for that is over, we've dealt with the past. This is a serious matter."

"Case?" I said.

She frowned. "Yes."

"What case? Where is this case you see, will you tell me, please? When the DeGrase baby was taken there were pieces that didn't fit, there were steps to follow; we caught the infant's aunt in lies and found out she'd snatched the kid and was blackmailing her own sister. We dug into their past and you stuck it out and kept coming at them from different angles until the woman broke. If Broghin and Lowell hadn't been tied up with the bank robbery at the time, they would've spotted it, too."

"We can only hope," Anna said. "But I still have my doubts about that. Don't underestimate your own temerity or the danger it placed you in at the time, as it has before."

"I don't want to go into it again."

"However, the fact remains that the police did not solve the case, and we did."

"That doesn't mean we should go hunting for trouble. There's nothing here involving us so far, just a lot of talk and rumor. You shouldn't get so caught up in playing Miss Marple."

Strands of her silver hair caught in the corners of her mouth, and she turned on me as I licked my milk mustache and made me think twice about my ability to outrun her.

Her hand shot out and gripped my wrist, and though her voice never wavered there was a pain in there that nearly took me out. "Are you suggesting I'm a senile woman who doesn't know the difference between reality and the irrational? That I cannot distinguish the truth from desultory fantasies?"

I swallowed thickly. "No, I'm not saying that. But I'm doing the dirty work to cover our asses and make sure Richie's corpse in the garbage doesn't really have anything to do with you."

She gave me a thick ha-rumph. "I do not need you to 'cover my ass.' In fact, the image is enough to give me chills. Kindly refrain." Anna worried her bottom lip and cleared her throat. "I've never seen you in this state. Obviously you have a great deal more than this" — she didn't use the word "case" — "situation weighing on your mind." She took a breath and held it longer than a champion diver, letting it out slow so that it puffed her hair back around her ears. "I am sorry I haven't noticed, that I've been preoccupied." She looked me in the eye and said quietly, "But you know that if you ever need to speak with me I am always available to you."

"I know. It's not your fault."

"Then, please, dear, tell me."

I didn't know what to say. "I'm getting a

little tired of it. I'm sick of always feeling like there's something chasing me. I'm not a cop or a private detective or a mystery writer who stumbles into real life crimes. I'm just a bookseller."

"Oh, you say that with such a sense of loss." She was taken aback and the sorrow lined her face. "You are far more than your designated career, Jonathan. You've proven that several times over the last half decade. You've a passion for justice surpassing that of most law officers. You also care about people, especially the people of this town."

"Of course I do," I said, "but that has nothing to do with this."

"It has everything to do with this."

"I'm not so sure."

"What happened today?" she asked.

"I'm not so sure about that, either," I said.

The sun had set and the kitchen had grown dark while we talked. I put on the light, a headache beginning to clamp the back of my skull.

Anna scratched her neck, leaving fine white line trails. "It's been a long time since you've been to the cemetery."

"Yes."

And that was that.

She said, "I'll get our dinner," and moved to the stove.

We ate lamb chops and Anubis eyed me woefully. I had a lot to talk about with Anna but didn't know how to begin again; she wouldn't push. I washed the dishes and took Anubis for a walk in the park and the two of us sat by the pond while the snow started to come down. When I got back I reread *Kosinski's Steps* and didn't like it as much the second time around. I got ready for bed and slept and woke in a dark fury, hearing my mother's neck crack, slept a little more, and woke again, the stitches pulling painfully whenever I turned in my sleep. My watch said 12:30. I got up.

Anna was in the kitchen, robe loose around her waist. "I couldn't do more than nap a half hour at a time," she said, "so I decided to make myself a hot cup of milk."

"People really drink it like that?"

She smiled. "Believe it or not, chemically it actually does help one get to sleep."

"I've already had my fill."

"As you wish."

I did not like the heavy politeness that had fallen between us, but couldn't think of a way to get past it. Maybe the morning would clear both our sensibilities.

She drank her milk. I started to ask about her day when she frowned at the same moment that Anubis cocked his head. "Did you hear something?" she asked.

"No."

"I could have sworn I heard a car door —"

She wheeled herself to the window and murmured my name.

Anubis barked twice.

"Oh shit," I said.

Anna looked back at me. Her right hand clawed the neck of her cardigan, face draining of blood until it was the color of her hair. Anubis barked twice more, sounding incredibly lethal. Anna's mouth thinned as if she champed at a bit, trying hard to swallow. She closed her eyes and kept them shut as she reached to pet Anubis, and he ducked his head beneath her hand and she opened her eyes and gazed steadily at me. "It seems we have quite a growing collection," she said. Her voice dropped like a boulder. Furrowed tracks ran across her forehead. She stroked the dog more firmly between the ears, and he began to whimper, then whine loudly, and I moved forward. "I think it's fair to say that we most certainly do have a case, Jonathan." She smiled faintly. "There's another body in the snow. A woman, I think."

10

Broghin and Lowell and the other cops ranged across the front yard as the snow spun madly. Red and blue lights flashed, and the wig-wag high beams threw hellish shadows against the brush. Neighbors came onto the sidewalks from both ends of the block, and the deputies asked questions and looked for a murder weapon all along the street. I sat at the top of the ramp watching the scene and feeling disconnected from it. I had a sour stomach. The headache was much worse. I bent and took a handful of snow and rubbed it into my face until I came a little of the way back.

The corpse was still there. They had set up a kind of lean-to over it to keep the snow off. They were taking photographs of it and every so often a powerful flash exploded and illuminated most of the yard. Jim Witherton's car went by slowly and Lowell stepped into the street and directed him to stop. They spoke for a couple of minutes and then shook hands and Lowell waved him on. Jim must've just gotten back from his night security shift at Syntech. He'd missed the action this time; he hadn't found our body tonight. I had.

I'd grabbed a flashlight and gone outside, and even before I saw her face I knew who it was. She was on her belly, one arm twisted around as if she was reading a good book on a beach and reaching to scratch her back. Her hand hung in the air, fingers splayed. Steam rose around her head. The light reflected off the thick lacquer of her turquoise nails: I hoped Mary Jean Resnick didn't spread the rumor that Anubis had partially eaten Karen Bolan, too.

Sheriff Broghin stepped beside me without a word. He stared long and hard and I stared back. He started to say something and then stopped, started and stopped again. His enormous gut hung out from beneath his jacket and over his belt like the blob trying to get at Steve McQueen. It was very close to the side of my head. He didn't cock his thumb and point his index finger. I rested my elbows on my knees and my chin on my fists. He said, "You . . ." and then cleared his throat and went into the house to talk with Anna.

Lowell tracked across the lawn, flipping a small notebook shut. "You're going to freeze out here not moving around," he said. "Let's go inside."

"I prefer to stay here."

"I don't. I've been going from a pizza oven to a refrigerator all day long and I can feel a goddamn head cold coming on."

"Too bad."

He breathed deeply and shook his head and put his notebook in his coat pocket. "You want to freeze your ass off, that's your business. Mine is to settle this."

"Hell of a job you've done so far," I said.

I wanted to snipe at somebody and now I'd done it to my friend, and it sure as hell didn't make me feel any better, especially when you considered the fact that he might break my arms now. The calm I'd seen drop over him at the Bubrick house in the afternoon descended once more like an avalanche. It was a bad thing to snipe at somebody who could look down death and not flinch, and I promised myself to remember it. I suddenly felt like I was stand- ing on an ice floe shattering beneath me, and a careless step in any direction would dump me in the bottomless ocean. He stood rigid as a statue of a Roman war god. An enraged bull wouldn't move him, or a tractor trailer or an air strike. Nothing except for one more wrong word from me, and then I'd need serious attention from the EMS.

"All right," I told him. "I'm sorry."

"Pull it together, Johnny," he said. "I don't need you in pieces. I'm not even sure I need you at all. You look like shit and you've been falling apart this whole time around, and now you're really starting to get on my nerves."

"Okay, okay, I already said I was sorry. What happened to her?"

He took off his hat and slapped it against his thigh, wiped sweat and snow off his forehead and put his hat on again. "Small caliber, maybe a twenty-two. In the ear."

"Christ."

"She was murdered someplace else and dumped here."

"It's becoming a regular habit for somebody."

He turned and looked at the other deputies checking the sewer drains and under nearby bushes. "She couldn't have been dead for more than a half hour. The bullet took out part of her head, but there's no sign of skull fragments or brain tissue in the vicinity. She might've even been shot right in the car and then thrown out. Blood was still running; it pooled beneath the body."

The body. Karen Bolan used to have a body, and now she simply was one — the body. No more ecstatic rubbing and hugging and overly loud and excited laughter; a lot of guys would miss out on her friendly flirting, her long legs drawing their attention. The widest cheesey smile was now gone forever, and I didn't have any idea why in the hell it had happened.

"Has anyone told Willie yet?" I asked.

"He's on a business trip in Houston, just flew down this afternoon, we checked first thing. Roy called there and got him out of bed and said the poor guy nearly fainted right on the phone. He's taking the first flight back, should be coming in at around eight this morning if the airport's not shut down by the blizzard. I'll meet him at the airport." Lowell clopped his boots against the porch stairs. "Goddamn awful way to find out. Now he'll feel wrong about it, guilty he wasn't here to watch over her."

"Hell, yes."

"Last night was the first time you've seen her in how long?"

"At least a year. Maybe longer. I think . . . I think it was at the winter carnival last year."

"How well did you know her?"

"As well as you. Probably less since I moved. What kind of question is that? I'm not up on recent events in her life, if that's what you mean, but she seemed the same as usual. You know what she's like."

"Yeah. She there when you had the fight with the guy with the crew cut?"

I nodded. "Like I said, I talked to her and Willie and Lisa and Doug Hobbes. Then I went looking for Tons Harraday, got caught up with the crew cut, and while we beat the crap out of each other she was there watching."

"She give any sign she knew this guy?"

"No."

He rubbed his eyes, turning it over in his head. There was nothing else you could do, wrapping yourself up in the knots and still finding that none of it made sense. "Those implications I told you about are becoming even more scattershot."

"You aren't kidding." I reviewed the questions — watching her there on the ground and waiting for her to move. "Where does Karen fit into all this? Does the guy with the crew cut tie her to this, and did he kill her, and Richie? Was the whole thing a set-up? Why?"

"I went to Jackals last night and asked around about the crew cut."

"Raimi's," I corrected. "And they sell Schlitz."

"It'll always be Jackals no matter how much money they sink into that hole. Only name for a bar that ever fit." He rested his

175

massive hands on the porch railing, and I could hear his shoulders crack as he shifted his weight from foot to foot. Snow clung to the edges of his face so that he looked like a Yeti. "The team had some good times there, though."

Some bad times too, I thought, but for once kept my mouth shut.

"Nobody knew the guy," he said. "Bartenders had never seen him in there before. Except for the crew cut and the smashed beer mug, nobody could really remember anything about him. They had their eyes on you because of the blood."

"That's a nice thought." I couldn't recall much either beyond the calm, crazy look in his eyes and my own heady rage. It had happened so fast. "He was nondescript," I said. "No outstanding features. He looked tough and mean in that calm insane way, written into his face. Had a perpetual sneer. He punched me in the forehead before I had a chance to really size him up, and then I was seeing stars more than anything else."

"But you would've taken him if he hadn't run."

I shrugged. Lowell glanced at the kitchen window and watched Broghin's shadow walk past the stove. I told him about my visit to the back hills and talking with Tons and

Deena and hunting around Richie's room.

"Yeah, I saw the rubbers, too," he said. "Kind of throws a new curve on it."

"Tons swears his brother never did enough so he would actually need a partner."

"I believe it. He was a real Momma's boy, Richie was, except he had no mother. Left him on a pretty short path."

"Was Margaret's jewelry ever found?" I asked.

"Yeah," he said. "We gave them back to her niece."

Two neighborhood kids had gone around through the park and were having a snowball fight across the street. Cops shooed them off but they didn't go far and started pelting one another with snowballs again, laughing, loudly, the way Karen would have. She was starting to freeze.

The snow fell harder, blanketing the areas where the ice had melted this afternoon. It was like watching somebody doing a paint-by-numbers where every number was white, covering over the haphazard patches. The wind returned, gusting across the skeletal branches of the canopy trees. The kids squealed and finally the cops shouted down the block to the parents and an embarrassed man in a ripped overcoat came and took the children home.

"Broghin's still a part of this," I said.

"Let's not start again."

"It's time to ask him some point-blank questions."

"Shooting at grizzlies will get you nowhere."

I burst out laughing. It hurt like hell, as if I'd forgotten how — and the stitches pulled — but I couldn't help it. Lowell didn't join in. The other cops stared. "Cripes. And you make fun of my lines."

He sighed. "Okay, it sounds dumb. But analogies aside, it's the truth. You get into his face and he'll get into yours. You want that? Anna has a lot more on the ball than you, Johnny, most of the time, and knowing her she's talking to him as his friend. She's got a better chance to learn what's been on his mind than either you or me. And I still don't think in the end it'll matter much. You don't trust him but I do, and that's the way it's got to be at the bottom line." A cruiser slowly pulled out into the street and blue light covered Lowell's face. "Shit, at least I didn't say 'you can catch more flies with sugar than vinegar.' "

He turned and spoke with the other deputies and ten minutes later Broghin came out and they all helped put Karen's body in Keaton Wallace's ME wagon. Then everybody left and I sat there and waited. I didn't know what I was waiting for. The wind tore a branch from the tip of a tree and it sailed across the rim of the thickets like a miniature witch's broom. The cops' tracks began to disappear. Before long the last trampled traces of where Karen's body had been were covered and filled in. The sky lightened with yellow and red. It kept snowing.

I kept waiting.

When I got out of bed it was nearly noon and my nose was running. I had a deep-rooted chill and shivered right through a twenty-minute hot shower. The swelling had gone down and the shiners were already fading. I had a date with Katie tonight and I wanted to look fairly presentable and take her someplace where they didn't sell Schlitz.

I called the store and got the answering machine. Debi must have had late classes, and if she didn't want to pull so many extra hours working, that was fine. I left a brief message and told her not to do anything vulgar with her boyfriend in front of the Brontë sisters. Hopefully, they were not already in the midst of such acts.

Anna was reading in the living room; I couldn't make out the title of the book because she'd taken the dust jacket off to keep from ruining it. Anubis trotted forward and stepped on my feet and urged me to take him for a walk in the park. I shoved him away and he shoved back, and we waltzed around like that for a while.

"Later," I told him. He gazed studiously at me as if he did not quite believe me but was willing to give me the benefit of the doubt. He hunkered down beside Anna, and she said, "Good morning."

I sat on the couch close to my grandmother and asked, "How are you?"

Anna smiled sadly. "I should be asking you that, dear. I didn't know the poor girl and you did. I'd ask you to tell me something about her but I fear that sounds too much like an interrogation at the moment. How do you feel?"

"Fine," I said.

She frowned and reached over and took my face in her hands the way Katie had yesterday morning. I liked when lovely women did that for me. "Your face is doing much better today. By the end of the week the bruises will be completely gone. Is your chest all right?"

I nodded. "Yes."

She shifted in her wheelchair and said, "Please save the pat answers, Jonathan. We

Kendricks are known for our stubbornness, not insensitivity, and especially not with each other. I saw you sitting on the porch last night alone and watchful like some dutiful soldier. In that terrible snow. It was nearly four-thirty when I went in to bed, and still you stayed. I've been worried about you."

"Anna, it's not that . . ." She made a hush sound. I suddenly wondered when I'd stopped calling her Grandma and why.

"I can only imagine what you were feeling all that time while they took so long examining your friend without even touching her. Good lord, so many pictures, the photographer must have taken hundreds. What do they need so very many for?"

I really hadn't considered what I was feeling, or what I wasn't feeling; the chill remained. Karen and I hadn't been close — never lovers or even truly good friends — but she was someone from my life, and to have her killed and thrown out on my lawn like a piece of trash . . . it struck at something in the same way it would everyone who knew her. Richie's death might've deserved my time and interest, but Karen's death deserved more. I wasn't certain what that was, or what I could do about it.

"I'm not sure," I said.

"I understand. As involved as we were in this before, the poor girl's murder . . ."

"Her name was Karen Bolan," I said.

Anna dropped her gaze and reached for a cup of tea on the bookstand. She knocked her book over and it fell between Anubis' paws. He drew back his head and peered down at the page so that it appeared he'd just read a story by Hemingway and was having trouble with the subtleties. I picked up the book and put it back on the stand. It was *The French Powder Mystery* by Ellery Queen.

"I know her name," Anna said. "I didn't mean to intimate that she had no identity."

"I know, I've just been taking semantics a bit too hard lately." I realized the abruptness of my remark. "I'm sorry." It seemed like I was apologizing a lot lately — and couldn't be sure if that was because I was letting my emotions get away with me or for the opposite reason. "I'm pissed off. I want to find the bastard who keeps using our yard like his own private cemetery. If it's that bastard with the crew cut I'm going to have to finish what he started." Anubis raised his head and jammed his nose beneath my hand. "I want to figure out if he's involved with these murders, and if so, why. If it's not him, I want to stop whoever keeps dragging us through this blood."

Anna saved her breath and simply said, "Yes."

"But I don't know how to do it. This one isn't like the others. This is striking too close to home, like with Mom and Dad. It's unnerving."

She took it in stride; my grandmother has an inexhaustible well of resolve. Unlike me, she never wavered, not in her beliefs or precepts. Self-doubt was as foreign to her as the far side of Venus.

"Do you believe Karen and Richie might have been directly or indirectly connected?"

I shrugged. "Connected? How so?"

"Involved," she said.

"Lovers?"

"It's a consideration."

Karen Bolan sleeping with Richie Harraday? I tried to picture it — the girl with the golden smile and the kid with sideburns using up his condoms. She certainly had the flirtatious nature for at least entrancing him into such a relationship. Could they have been screwing around in Willie's bed while he was away on business, or would Richie have taken her fishing at the river like a couple of infatuated young sweethearts, or would Karen have taken him shopping at Victoria's Secret?

"I'm having a hard time with that one," I

said. "Karen openly flirted with everyone. She may have had lovers on the side, I wouldn't be surprised, but Lowell said Richie was more or less a Momma's boy. Karen's playful, aggressive forwardness probably would have scared him off. Not that they would have ever traveled in the same circles to begin with."

"No one thought the boy could burglarize a home, either."

"Deena told me he had his secrets."

"Even after his demise," she added.

And what were Broghin's? "What did the sheriff have to say last night?"

"Pertaining to this case, very little."

"Exactly how little is little?"

"He asked the questions that were to be expected," she said. "If I had heard anything, if I knew the deceased, etcetera. We drank a cup of coffee and he spoke on at length about Clarice and his children. He certainly is in love, though I'm curious as to what prompted him to go on in that vein, considering last night's circumstances."

A black thought creeping towards me finally sprang. Broghin had been acting so unglued and weird lately that I wondered if, after dealing with the underside of a sleepy town and seeing the rot that infected it beneath its pretty gingerbread borders, the gate to his own ugly side had lifted, and he was committing these murders himself.

Anna's gaze tangled with mine. "You're right to be suspicious, but whatever has been bothering Sheriff Broghin, I can assure you he is certainly not who we are looking for."

"You can't guarantee that."

"I can adamantly —"

"There are no assurances."

She knew I was talking about Phillip Dendren, whom we had both loved. She shook her head testily, looked up and scanned the various frames on the wall for my parents. The photographs were more than family, friends and the past; the collage stood as a testament to a world when the illusion of implicit trust still existed.

"Broghin said nothing else?" I asked.

"Hardly."

"Doesn't he have any leads at all? Suspects? Anything? I figured you would have squeezed him for all the information you could have."

"One would think." She smiled pleasantly. "Perhaps I've become too convivial in my later years."

"He's a part of this, Anna."

"Hm."

"He knows more than he's telling."

"I will agree to that, but I don't believe that constitutes his being personally involved in this case. He's afraid of something, and it is that fact, in itself, that disturbs me more than anything else thus far. There may be no assurances in life, but I have known him for much of my life, and he deserves more than a modicum of respect."

Lowell wasn't giving me the help I needed, and I wasn't getting anywhere fast by myself. Miss Marple and Ellery Queen would've found a bloody dagger, a piece of string, a burnt match in an ashtray, and the case would be solved quite conveniently. They would round up a short list of suspects and make them all sit in the library while they proceeded to expose the culprit. The killer would be revealed, and at that point make a brief struggle before confessing and being politely escorted out. There would be no hard feelings.

My stupid list didn't have so much as a name on it anymore. I decided to tell Anna about the note — the letter which may or may not have been written by Broghin's wife, and which may or may not have been left on Richie Harraday's corpse — who may or may not have been murdered — depending on which cop you spoke to, and when, and whether or not you had ever thrown a chair at his head.

She reacted the way I expected her to. Her silver eyebrows arched demoniacally in a respectable imitation of Jack Nicholson. I explained about the dry spot on Richie's leg, Lowell's misgivings and then his sudden turnaround. She nodded sagely and her features hardened. I could take a lecture, but I didn't want to hear one precisely at this moment. Her hand found Anubis' snout and her fingers brushed back and forth across his nose until he went into a sneezing fit.

"Why didn't you mention this to me sooner?"

"Because I'm still not sure what it means, if it means anything at all."

"But you feel it does. And rather than bring it to my attention and discuss this aspect of the case you decided to remain silent."

Case. I was really starting to hate that word. "Lowell says —"

She gave an exasperated huff. "Deputy Tully is obviously having a personal conflict, split between his loyalties and his honor. Anyone can see he's a man who deeply loves his job, his fellow officers, and his neighbors, and is not always capable of placing one in front of the other, as his duty calls for." She spoke as if she knew him well, and could easily break down his personality into the sum of his traits; but Lowell wasn't a man you could claim did much by way of the obvious. "You chose to keep me unaware of the note because you wanted to protect me."

"Yes."

"I don't enjoy the idea of you working on your own agenda, Jonathan. How do you expect to protect me when you keep me in the dark?"

"That's not true. I've told you nearly everything, there just hasn't been much."

She took a sip of her tepid tea and coughed and placed the cup down roughly. Tea spilled onto Anubis' back and he got up and sat behind her wheelchair, sick of getting things dropped on him. "Clarify it for me, Jonathan, if you feel that I'm not quite sharp enough to be told the full extent of what's occurred."

"You don't want it clarified."

She stared flatly at me. "What are you insinuating by that?"

"Nothing."

"Another safe, pat answer."

I reached over and held up *The French Powder Mystery*. "It's not as cut and dried as this, Anna. On the one hand, you're the strongest, smartest person I've ever known, out on the other you allow yourself to allow your natural nosiness to turn awful events into charming entertainment. It's not about solving riddles and puzzles. It's about digging into lives and raking muck and dealing with somebody who could put a twenty-two in a lady's ear and pull the trigger, and maybe finding out that somebody you cared about is capable of killing your parents. Yes, I want to watch over and protect you. You say Broghin being frightened disturbs you — well, how's it make you feel that I'm on the cusp of being fairly terrified myself?"

She enunciated quite carefully. "Jonathan, it is a part of life."

"Ah, only if you're lucky."

"I believe you are in sore need of clarification yourself. I read mysteries because I enjoy them. I do not spend my days fantasizing that I am a detective, or that you are my sidekick, for that matter. Do not put such emphasis on my attitude." She wheeled forward. "Rather accept your own." Almost as an afterthought she added, "And in case you've forgotten, I do happen to know something of death."

"I haven't forgotten," I said. "I'd just like to get some distance."

She kissed me on the cheek, took my dirty plate and cup and put them in her lap, then went to the kitchen. She filled the sink with soapy water and began washing the dishes and pans while I stared at her back wondering if anything had been resolved. There was a knock at the door.

I looked outside; the window was too thick with rime and snow to see anyone. I called Anubis with a firm order. Even in his most temperamental moods he'll do what I say when I use that tone of voice. He shot up and stood beside me. For perhaps the hundredth time I wished I didn't hate guns so much that I didn't own one. I opened the door.

Two adolescent girls with snow shovels stood at attention just a hair less rigid than a pair of marines. They were ready to work. One wore a perfectly fitted pink ski suit that would have made an Olympic skier proud, and the other had on white ear muffs, a powder-puff coat, cross-threaded boots and tight leather gloves. They had stern faces and red cheeks.

The first girl said, "We're going to shovel the walk for Mrs. Kendrick now, okay?"

"Okay," I said.

"It's still snowing so we might be back later to go over it again, okay?"

"Okay."

They looked confused and didn't move.

The weight of the economic recession bore down on them.

"Do you want money now?" I asked. I didn't know what kind of an arrangement Anna had established with them, whether she prepaid them for the season or what.

"Yes, please," the one with ear muffs said.

I opened the storm door, took out my wallet and gave them ten bucks. The girl held it by the corner as if it were actually roadkill with a picture of Alexander Hamilton on it.

"More?" I asked.

"Yes, please," she said.

They were polite extortionists. I handed the girl in the pink ski outfit another ten. They each put the bills in identical change purses that contained no change but lots of wadded bills. The lowest denomination I saw was a twenty. The girls started shoveling the porch and ramp. They were a great deal more skilled at the job than I was, hurling shovelfuls of wet snow over their shoulders and chopping down to crack four-inch layers of ice. If they'd heard what had transpired last night they didn't let it impede their performance.

"Cripes, kids are serious nowadays."

I hopped up and sat on the kitchen

counter the way I used to when I was a boy; perhaps I was trying to regain my youth when I did not have to pay two girls twenty bucks to shovel the walk, when I myself did the same to the tune of only fifty cents and felt helplessly ripped off.

"At least we now have a definite course of action," Anna told me.

"Yeah, to sell the shop and start shoveling driveways for a living."

She grinned. "Christine and Josepha do attack their chosen profession with a great deal of verve."

"They can afford to. So what's our course of action?"

"The letter may be nothing, as Deputy Tully suggested, but he admits he did not read its entire contents. Something within that note may shed a new light. We have to read it."

"And how do you propose we do that?"

She pursed her lips. "In this instance I truly believe honesty is the best policy," she said. "I will ask him. And I am confident he will tell me what he's been hiding. He was prepared to do so last night, but I couldn't help him get over the initial hurdle." She gave me a puzzled frown. "Why you decided to let Lowell wait is beyond me. I don't share your patience."

"But you've got conviviality."

"Barrels of it."

I got down from the counter and put on my coat.

Anna raised a soapy hand and pointed at me. "I suggest you let me speak with the sheriff alone, Jonathan. If you two start irritating one another even more than usual we'll never get anywhere."

"I'll leave that part of it to you, Anna. I admit you can handle Broghin much better than me. But I still have to go talk with somebody."

Maybe we'd managed to get a handhold on enough threads of the tapestry — now I had to use them, tie knots and set a snare. It was time to start pushing harder and shove the killer out into the open, and hopefully be nowhere near when it happened.

"Who?" she asked.

"Lisa Hobbes might know if Karen was having an affair with Richie or if they had some other tie." I opened the front door and Anubis raced forward, and when I pressed him back he gave me a hurt look of betrayal. "If Lisa doesn't know then I suppose I'll have to go ask Mary Jean Resnick."

11

Lisa and Doug Hobbes' house sprawled at the top of Saint Gabriel Court, not far from the Corner Convenience. It was a split-level ranch with intricate brick work trim, wood pattern shingles, and high tech aerials to nab cable channels from Buenos Aires. Lisa's yellow El Dorado sat shining in the driveway.

When they were newlyweds they started out in the basement of Doug's father's house and eventually bought the place from his dad when the old man moved to Florida. Doug's father had been our little league coach for our worst season: one and nineteen. We even lost against the Prospect County Indians for the first time in twenty-five years; Doug's dad got into a couple of brawls with steel mill workers who didn't take losing to the Prospect County Indians too well, and much to our relief that ended his dubious career as a little league coach.

Lisa liked cats. There were three in view, wandering the yard, slinking over the chain-link fence and poking through the small doorway of the shed, straw and detris clinging to their whiskers. They lived out-doors all year round and grew thick layers of fat and fur in the winter.

I rang the bell and could hear a faint *ding dong* within. As I waited, two of the cats sauntered up the stoop and made figure eights around my legs, mewling loudly. I rang the bell again and only more cats came. Four of them now. I stopped ringing the bell. They smelled badly, not dirty but strangely clean, antiseptic. I didn't dislike cats but I hated to see whole packs of them. It reminded me of the unbalanced elderly ladies in the city who take in dozens of strays until the health department is finally forced to remove them.

I turned and started back to the Jeep and the front door opened. It took Lisa about ten seconds to focus on me. Her mouth gnarled into a stunted smile. She wore baggy jeans and an incorrectly buttoned white blouse, and she looked like a brick wall had toppled on her. Her eyes were ex-tremely red, with brutal dark circles under them. She had her hair pulled back in a messy pony tail that left as many tufts out of the rubber band as tucked in.

"Johnny," she said.

Seeing her, it hit me how wrong I was to come here and churn questions. Lisa and

Karen had been close friends since before kindergarten. For them it had always been a case of opposites attracting — hushed and loud, small and tall, extrovert and introvert. Now Lisa seemed halved. They had been a proper pair counterbalancing each other. Karen had once almost knocked Doug on his ass in study hall because he'd been too shy to ask Lisa to the homecoming dance. When he finally did ask, she'd been too timid to say yes. Karen wound up having to connive a ride from Doug and virtually flinging them together on the gym floor.

Lisa watched over Karen too, who enjoyed playing devil's advocate far too much for her own good. Before she'd married Willie, her flirting had on occasion tempted too many rednecks into the fold. The summer after graduation, she cut out the back of Jackals to smoke a joint in some guy's car and a half hour later came running in bleeding from her nose and mouth, naked from the waist up. I didn't know the guy and she didn't press charges and he supposedly split for greener pastures soon thereafter. She settled down with Willie that autumn, but being the center of attention meant a lot to her. She always said she wanted to be a comedienne. And she couldn't forgo the thrill she got from wiggling smoothly under male noses and laughing so loudly the whole room was forced to turn and look.

Had she done it that night at Raimi's?

My voice was thick, the words inane. "How are you doing, Lise?"

"Come in," she said, and I walked in and shut the door. "You look full of intent. What can I do for you?" Her bottom lip gave out immediately and she started crying. We stepped close together in the foyer and hugged, and her whole body shook as though she would shatter in my arms. I muttered worthless sentiments and she nodded and sobbed. We stayed like that for a long time.

She sniffled and said, "I'm sorry."

"Don't be."

"It's just that . . ."

"You don't have to explain."

It smelled antiseptic in the living room, too; she'd been dusting, mopping with detergent, polishing, washing dishes, keeping herself busy. Housewives in pain had nowhere to go but deeper into their houses. A vacuum leaned against the coffee table. Her wedding album and high school yearbook lay open on the couch. There was a box of tissues on the table. She took one and wiped her eyes and blew her nose softly.

"I want some tea," she said, laughing the way people will after choking on tears.

"Would you like a cup?"

I couldn't think of anything I wanted less at the moment than tea, except maybe for decaffeinated coffee. "Yes," I said. "Please."

"I only have herbal."

"Whatever you're having is fine."

"Camomile it is."

She put on the pot, and I paged through the wedding album. I liked her gown but thought the bridesmaid dresses were garish. Only Karen looked good in hers. I opened our yearbook and scanned some of the comments Lisa's friends had written. Most of them had so many inside jokes and high school jargon they were unintelligible. I read my own remarks and didn't remember any of the things I'd been referring to.

Lisa entered with a tray of cookies, pie and tea. She tried pouring me a cup, but her hand shook and the hot water splashed. I took the kettle from her.

She glanced down at the albums and said, "Lot of memories in those."

"For me, too."

"You didn't come to my wedding, did you?"

"I couldn't." She'd been married somewhere in the middle of my three-month jail term.

"Yes, that's right." She pushed some pilows aside and sat. She shoved the plate of cookies at me. "I hope you like chocolate chip. Doug doesn't, but I'm addicted and they were on sale. There are some Oreos, too, in the cupboard, if you'd like."

"No, Lise, thanks. Please, relax."

She smiled and frowned at once, features tugging. Too much, too soon. "Well, you start on those. I'd like to freshen up, Johnny, and then we'll talk."

"Okay," I said.

She was gone ten minutes and returned more in control of herself. The blouse had been buttoned properly and she wore a fashionable blue belt. She'd let her hair loose and brushed it into her usual style. She had on light makeup, and the color was back in her face. "I felt even more horrendous than I looked, which is really saying something. People have been calling and dropping by all morning but I didn't want to see anybody, really. I've been cleaning all day, everything. I grouted the upstairs bathroom, can you believe it? I've never bothered, and now I know it's even worse than I thought. Doug is the neatness fanatic."

"Where is he?" I asked.

"Over in Buffalo," she said. "He left yesterday afternoon to wine and dine some valuable clients."

"I thought he was manager of the men's retail store over at the mall in Prospect."

"No, Willie got him a job at Syntech eight months ago. Don't ask me what he does. He's told me but I don't understand any of his computer jargon, and I should because I'm getting left at the wayside. It started off as a hobby a couple of years ago and now he could be building a space station for all I know." She grinned. "He called twice yesterday afternoon. He usually calls in the afternoon, but not yet today. I never thought to ask him for the name of his hotel or room number. I mean, I never needed to reach him before. You're always supposed to have the name of the hotel in case of an emergency, but who actually thinks that way?"

I could think of about a million people with beepers who never liked to be out of contact for an instant.

"Lowell called and said he and that other deputy, Roy, were going to pick him up at the airport this morning. There's a blizzard in Buffalo and the flights are probably either cancelled or delayed." She absently ran her fingers along the edge of the tissue box. "He's due tomorrow, and I'm sure Willie could use lots of friends soon. Not right now, but soon. I haven't phoned him yet. To tell you the truth, I'm afraid I won't be able to say anything. I'm afraid I'll make it worse."

"You won't, but I can understand." I took a sip of tea. It was like drinking diluted cough syrup.

"You're so sweet, Johnny." Her voice took on the same sense of importance it had the other night. "We're all proud of you, you know. I've never had a chance to say it to your face before, but the way you've handled yourself since your parents were killed . . . we admire what you've done, how you caught that man, and a few others like him over the years, and I know the DeGrases owe you everything."

"Lise . . ."

"You don't like talking about it, I'm sorry. So tell me, outside of the obvious, why are you here?"

"I wanted to ask some questions about Karen."

"Why?"

How to answer that: *Because your murdered best friend might've been screwing a kid burglar who may have caused the death of Margaret Gallagher and . . . ?* Two people had been killed in less than a week and left on my lawn and more lives might be on the line, not the least of which being Anna's and my own. I just didn't know. The extent of how much I didn't know was intimidating. Proper etiquette and tactfulness went out the window. "It's important," I said.

"All right. What do you want to ask, Johnny?"

"You know Karen was found on my grandmother's yard."

"Yes. My God, it's terrible. Just like that boy."

I nodded. "His name was Richie Harraday. Have you ever heard of him before?"

"No."

"Karen never mentioned him?"

"No."

"Are you sure?"

"It's not a difficult question," she said. "I'm sure she never mentioned him." Lisa frowned. "Unless you mean after this Richie guy was already dead. Then, well, you heard her, she was talking about your dog eating him and stuff . . ."

"I meant before. I was just wondering if she knew him. If she ever mentioned him."

"No, never. But why would . . . ?" Lisa paused. She reached for a cookie and absently nibbled off a few crumbs and then looked at it as if she'd been eating raw sewage and put it down. Her voice shrank further and tears filled her eyes but tenaciously held on and didn't fall. "Why would he kill her? And like that, in the same manner? On your lawn?" She stared at me. "What do you have to do with this, Johnny?"

Anna's van was gone and Anubis was still giving me dirty looks. I put on my sweats to take him to the park when I decided to try Jim Witherton again. He was the only person somehow related to Richie Harraday's murder who I hadn't spoken to. Out on the lawn, Anubis sniffed at the spot where Karen's corpse had been found so close in time and place to Richie's and then searched my face for answers. He kept hoping, and when he realized I had none he went back to sniffing. I tugged him on and we jogged up the block. I rapped sharply on Jim's storm door, and it nearly fell off the same way the Bubricks' had. The windows were dark with heavy drapes and yellowed shades, the kind of decor only a confirmed bachelor would ever choose, or not having chosen, still live with because it didn't matter enough.

Jim answered the door wearing a burgundy terrycloth robe and insulated white socks with holes in them. His toenails were sharp enough to fend off a wolf. His black hair hung in lengthy ringlets to the middle of his back. He was freshly shaven and smelled of Aqua Velva. He had a half-eaten piece of buttered toast in his hand — edges daintily cut off — and after he finished swallowing said, "Jon."

"Sorry to bother you, Jim."

He had one of those small smiles that started and ended at one corner of his mouth. "No bother at all, believe me. I'm kind of glad you stopped by. I was just wasting the day before my shift. Come on in. I don't think that dog likes me."

"He doesn't like anybody."

"You can leave him out there then."

I ordered Anubis to sit and stay. He gave me a wry look that said I shouldn't bother him with petty commands, but he didn't mind so long as he was out of the house. He lay on Jim's welcome mat and rolled onto his side with a grunt and stared off at a series of faint tracks in the snow heading towards a clump of spruces.

Jim was only a few years older than me, but his mannerisms made him seem almost elderly. There was a slight hitch in his walk and he moved slowly, stoop-shouldered. He coughed constantly, his chest as resonant as a cave, and although he remained relatively thin he still sort of waddled.

"My sleep is all screwed up," he said. "I

can't get used to these times. You know when you have to change the clocks, you're screwed up for a few days? It's like that for me almost all the time. Even when I get home at one or two in the morning I can't manage to sleep. It's like six in the evening for everybody else, except there's nothing to do. Even the bars are closing. And you can forget about watching TV, all they have are these infomercials and sex phone ads. You ever call one a them?"

"No."

"They ain't so good, believe me. It's a wonder the Moral Majority don't come down harder on them. And they cost a bundle. You ever work a night shift?"

"In college," I said. "I was a bartender for a while."

He nodded and looked at his feet and tried to work his big toe back into his sock. "I can guess what you want to talk about." He nodded some more and I nodded with him because it seemed the thing to do. "Another one last night. We oughtta be ashamed what's happening in this town."

"Tell me what happened the night you found Richie Harraday's body."

He sighed and rubbed at the indents of his eyes. "Not much to tell, and what there was, I already told to the cops, believe me. I didn't exactly find the body, I just saw it lying there. Wasn't sure what it was at first, and then I realized. Scared the piss out of me is what it did, to be honest. I ran to your grandmother's house as much for my own sake as hers. I didn't know if somebody was still prowling around or what. Could've been seven psychos out there waiting to jump me. Freaked me pretty bad."

"Anna appreciated you staying with her."

"I appreciated her not sending me home," he said, laughing.

"Did you see anything on his body?"

Jim's forehead creased and he gave me a sidelong glance. "Lowell asked me the same question last night when I drove by. Now why do you ask that?" I didn't say anything. "Just snow."

"No footprints? Tire tracks? Nothing else?"

"Just snow. It was coming down hard that time of night, the way it has most of the week. That's why I didn't recognize him — it, I guess I should say — as a body. Looked weird and I was kind of bored, like I mentioned, and decided to come back and take a look. Nothing else to it, believe me."

"Thanks for telling me," I said. I hadn't thought he'd have anything new to add, but I'd been compelled to question him myself.

I believed him almost as much as he seemed to want me to.

He shook his head. "Why would anybody want to do that to a nice girl like Karen Bolan, huh? The guy I heard was a burglar and a real creep, but why would anybody hurt that lady?"

"I didn't realize you knew Karen," I said.

Back to nodding. "Sure, sure, I know Willie from when he works late at night, which is almost always. He's a hustler that guy. Puts in a hell of a lot of overtime but it's really paid off for him. He'll make senior VP within the next couple of years, you watch. You want a beer or somethin'?"

"No thanks."

"Yeah, her and Willie made a nice couple. A little weird, you know, what with the strong personalities if I dare say, but nice. She sometimes picked him up or brought him a late snack. Always had a nice word to say to me at the door. Never minded signing in or putting on the visitors badge the way they're supposed to, even if she was only gonna stay a minute. A real golden smile on that lady." After a pause he added, "How's your grandmother holding up?"

"She's doing good," I said. Jim Witherton, security guard and green toenail grower *extraordinaire,* was not a professional bodyguard or a martial artist, but I would not have wanted Anna to be alone that night. For all I knew, there *were* still seven psychos running around loose. "Thanks for all your help. Some people might not have gotten involved."

"That's New York City you're talking about," he said. "This is still Felicity Grove, believe me."

We shook hands and said good-bye, and Anubis bounded at my heels and we ran back up the block and around to the main gate of the park.

Jim was right.

It was always Felicity Grove; with its cool mint ambiance, park and children, ring of oak trees near the courthouse with initials and hearts with arrows through them carved in as far back as 1890. Aging and fertile. The lake where seniors rented boats on prom night before driving up to the back woods, where I'd lost my virginity like everyone else. With the memorial plaques and statues of historical figures that sparked no recognition: who could possibly know the civil war hero *Orville Drinkle?* The high school was like a social machine where we had been turned out with as many hopes as fears, and too many good yearbook photos, all of us stuck together by that selfsame glue of youth no matter how much time passed. The inevitable snowfall followed by the five ton sanders, red-eared children with ski suits and shovels trying to make a few bucks, and succeeding. Thick-furred dogs barking behind low wooden fences, cats forever mewling in trees — the fire department really did climb ladders to save them — girls skipping rope and running garage sales beside their mothers, and paper boys riding bikes across the neighborhood, perfecting their boomerang *Gazette* underhand toss.

It was always Felicity Grove.

With its shadows and dead and filthy secrets.

Home.

I let Anubis romp loose. Kids were sledding along some of the slopes and twenty or thirty people skated on the lake. I felt like going out there and unwinding but I'd left my skates at my apartment.

Anubis cut left towards the trees and sped through the snow, sliding and kicking out clumps. I jogged along the running paths; the thick evergreens and pines acted like umbrellas to keep the powdered trails passable. I usually ran in Central Park at least once a week, but my legs and back were especially stiff today. Nothing a beautiful oriental masseuse with teak wood sandals couldn't fix.

I tried to keep a steady pace, but the tightness in my stitched chest kept throwing off my stride, ice so bad in spots I had to stop and carefully walk past. The trail rose across a ridge of copses and fell away to the distant side of the lake. There was nobody else at this end of the park. The virgin snow proved I was the only one willing to give it a shot. Orville Drinkle would have been proud.

It took twenty minutes to finish one complete circuit of the park, and I wasn't certain if I wanted to do a second. I passed Anubis sitting in the remains of a children's snow fort. He got up and started running with me and dropped off after a quarter mile. Kids knew his name and called to him and he charged through the brush. I kept going and started getting my second wind ten minutes later as I came up the ridge again. Tobacco was suddenly strong in the fresh air. Wind pressed it at me, and I peered around but didn't see anyone until the guy with the crew cut was nearly on top of me.

"Okay," I said.

I should've noticed his tracks even though he'd come from the opposite direction. The rest happened fast: he stepped out from behind the trees and spit his cigarette at me; I stopped short and ducked instinctively as he swung a Bowie knife downward at my legs. If I'd taken another step he would have sheared through my thigh. I shoved him hard and took an off-balance swing at his chin. I missed and followed through so far I knocked him down and tripped over him, hoping he'd dropped the blade. We both scrambled to our feet, five yards apart. He was on the path beneath the trees and I stood below him at the top of the slope, calf-deep in a dune of snow drift.

"Stupid to bring a guard dog and then let him run so far," he said. He held the knife confidently and comfortably, out near his fingertips, ready. His wrist was taped.

"Did you kill Richie?" I asked.

"No use in talking."

"And Karen, too? Why?"

"Still asking questions, even now? Damn, you're insane, boy."

"Look who's talking."

He must have hated me in his bones to want to carve me up so badly when he could've just used the .22 he'd killed Karen with. Maybe he didn't trust it unless he could place it in my ear, too. I might've been able to outrun him, if I'd been in-clined to. I wasn't. I wanted to smash his teeth down his throat so badly my hands itched. I whistled loudly, a short, high note that carried across the park.

"He'll kill you when he gets here," I said.

Crewcut knew how to use the blade and he was eager to get at me, holding the knife up in front now, weaving it through the air like a snake mesmerizing its prey. He wasn't a redneck joker who could only gut fish and skin small animals. His smile was vapid, calm eyes containing levels of madness, and although his face remained equally nondescript, something chimed. "Maybe you'll be dead by then."

"We already played this out once," I said.

"It's going to be different."

He took a step forward and I moved to his right, snow soaking through my sweats and chilling my legs. Miss Marple would've been able to talk herself out of this situation but all I could think of were more questions. "Who the hell are you?"

Like the last time we'd fought, he didn't waste his breath in dialogue. He rushed me, arcing the Bowie towards my belly. I tried to backpedal and couldn't find any purchase on the slope; heels digging in, I moved to my left and kept from tumbling. Instead of tagging my stomach he overshot and crashed into me and we both dropped backwards over the edge, sliding along the snowy copse. We wrestled and rolled end over end for a hundred feet, with him trying to stab me in the legs on the way down.

I looked up into his mouth; his back teeth were brown nubs. "Why didn't you stay out of it?" he said.

"Why'd you drag me into it?"

"You did this. You made it happen."

I grabbed his bad wrist and squeezed. He groaned and spun and wouldn't let go of the knife. With his free hand he punched me in the hinge of my jaw where the nerve center is and my head exploded. I cried out but kept squeezing harder and harder. Kids were yelling in the distance. Bones crackled as I crushed the wrist. He screamed and I liked the sound of it. He clubbed me across the neck and we dragged each other to the edge of the lake. The knife fell into the snow and I hauled him over my chest, rolling to get him away from it. He wound up on top. There was a lot of blood soaking through from the reopened slash on my chest, the snow changing to pink. Flat on my back he straddled me and screamed, "It was an accident, you nosy asshole! It had nothing to do with you!" He dug through the snow, searching for the blade, straining to reach forward as I pulled him back, and he found and grasped the knife handle.

Anubis leaped and tore out his throat.

12

More of the same.

Cops at work, the crowd and little kids watching, with me standing in the middle of it all, feeling nothing and not quite ashamed of my detachment. It had been almost two hours, and Anubis wouldn't leave my side. The blood and excitement made him nervous, and he kept licking his lips, eyes flitting from face to face. He growled whenever anyone came near. The cops didn't know whether to give him a medal or gas him. Roy wanted to ask me a question, but as he approached he regarded the dog, swallowed audibly, shut his mouth and turned away. The police photographer took another hundred pictures of another corpse. I wondered if I'd be arrested.

The temperature had dropped to the teens and Broghin kept sweating, face crimson with the exertion from walking up and down the slope.

"Okay," he said, "go through it once more." Bing's "White Christmas" played on in my head. "From the beginning." Again there was no anger in him today, but at least he didn't come across with that ridiculous caring uncle attitude he'd taken the other evening.

What had been resolved for him?

"I've told you twice already," I said.

"Tell me again."

"First get me a jacket or let me go home and grab one. I'm wet and freezing."

Broghin must've enjoyed using the walkie-talkie affixed to his belt because he called Roy on it when the deputy was only ten yards behind him. Roy went to his cruiser, opened the trunk and brought me a spare coat.

"Don't I get a plastic badge and a two-way wrist radio?" I asked.

Roy smirked and said, "You pick some damn strange times to tell jokes, don't you?"

Wallace examined the body, making notes on the tracks and angles of bloodshed. Like a fire hose, crew cut's severed carotid artery had spurted his steaming blood over my shoulder to where it had melted through the ice and refrozen at the lip of the lake. Lowell and four other deputies were holding the people back.

I told the sheriff the story again. I got the sense that he wasn't listening to me for yet the third time. He kept looking down at the dog with a mixture of anxiety and pride, and fussed with sweaty strands of his hair. More than anything he seemed to exude satisfaction and relief.

"Why are you so happy?" I asked.

Chins jiggling, Broghin did a double take, the blue-black veins at his temples knotting. Still none of his usual gruffness came through. " 'Cause my Preparation H is working today, and with you I need it full strength."

That was a fairly good comeback for him. I let it pass. "Who was he?"

Broghin didn't like being questioned, and for a moment the glare returned but faded immediately, replaced by an odd solace. "John Doe so far. No identification on him. We lifted his prints but he's not on file, and that dog didn't leave much for us to take a picture of and fax."

Crew cut was commonplace, an Everyman with a profound rage. Even now I checked him to remind myself this had happened, that the same person remained there. "Nobody's missing anything," I said.

"He is," Broghin said. "His face."

"Did you find a car? He's either parked in the lot or in the woods. Or else somebody dropped him off."

"Thanks for letting me know that,"

Broghin said. "Never would have thought of that on my own. Might be he parked on a nearby street. We'll get right on it and check. I appreciate you reminding me what my job is."

It must be the Lake Effect that makes everybody in this town so hyper-sensitive. "Don't you have any idea who he might be?"

"No." The word was bitten off from a great deal more left to be said.

I could've pushed — insulted, argued, or coaxed — and perhaps I would've, except news trucks were pulling up behind the rinky-dink orange sawhorse barricade. Video cameras zoomed in all over the scene, getting close-ups of the body and trying to get a shot of me and Anubis. We were adequately shielded so long as the sheriff stood in front of us.

Wallace Keaton trudged from the corpse as the EMS put the body in the hearse. He grinned painfully, thumb pressed against his gums and shoving at his bottom dentures. Broghin grimaced. "Wallace, you look like a damn fool with your fingers always in your mouth."

"Pardon me for speaking my mind, sheriff," Wallace muttered, "but go shit in your hat. I've been on my feet for thirty hours. Last night I had to do an autopsy on a girl who's mother is an hysterical wreck and near ready for the friggin' funny farm. Now I have to go back for this son of a bitch, who may have killed her."

"We don't know that for certain. Christ, don't go spewing conjecture when the press is just waiting to jump. What have you got for me?"

"For you? What in the hell do you think I got for you? A Caucasian male approximately twenty-five years old, and lived about half a second with his throat ripped out. That's all I'm going to have until I get him on the table, and I doubt there will be anything much more substantial then. What do you got, Frank? I thought the police would have had these matters resolved by now."

Lowell came over and said something to Broghin, and the sheriff gave me and Wallace a final glance before stalking off to make a statement to the reporters. Wallace said, "I had a terrible feeling you were going to become involved in this, Jon."

His face was so long beneath the terrier moustache I almost laughed. "They weren't just my grandmother's inclinations, Wallace."

He went after his back teeth again, prodding and tugging, and said, "I understand," though he looked extremely confused. I hoped he'd go to a new dentist soon. "You're bleeding. Lift your shirt, let me take a look."

I carefully pulled my sweatshirt over my head, and the throbbing flames dancing along my chest sprouted into all-out pyrotechnics.

"These stitches have pulled," he said, touching them gingerly. "Could've been a lot worse. Goddamn, I can't tell if you're the luckiest guy in the world or if you've got a home lined with broken mirrors." He plucked at the thread. "Go in and have them redone no later than tomorrow."

"Sure."

Wallace crossed the snowy field to his wagon, and the police parted the crowd to let him drive through with crew cut's corpse.

Lowell handed me his hat and said, "Here, you'll catch pneumonia."

I put it on and wasn't surprised to discover that a family of four could have lived comfortably inside. "Do I get my plastic badge and two-way wrist radio now?"

He ignored me. "I don't know who spread the word already but the big newspapers got hold of your name. I have no idea how they arrived here so quickly, but they're waiting to talk to you."

"Not again."

"Yeah, I know how well you get along with hordes of pretty reporters sticking microphones in your face."

"Depends on how pretty they are," I said, scanning the crowd. "Is the blonde from channel thirty-five around? The one with the cute overbite?"

"Yep," he said, "and not only is she more attractive but she's more polite than the rest, too. Handed me her card and requested that I ask you to do a formal interview." He took it out of his pocket and handed it to me.

"Hm. How formal do you think she means?"

"I'd say very. She's got a rock on her ring finger the size of a Buick."

I gave the card back to him.

He looked at it for a second and crumpled it, knuckles cracking, and let it fall. "What a mess."

"Did you pick up Willie?"

"Yeah."

"How's he doing?"

Lowell squinted into the flashing lights and cameras. "A zombie," he said. "He's all brass on the outside but he's tin in the center. He and Karen were close but they never seemed to rely on each other much, always did their own thing. Sometimes those are the ones who depend on one another the most, down at the bottom, where it counts."

"Where is he now?"

"He didn't want to go back to the house. Couldn't face that yet. His folks are dead and no other relatives live in the county, so I brought him to the Hobbes'. Doug is out of town until tonight, but at least he's got Lisa."

"She'll help," I said.

He turned to the kids playing in the fields. Some skaters were practicing double axels on the far end of the lake. "I could have Roy run you home."

"I think that would be best."

"Me, too."

Roy was not thrilled to have Anubis in his cruiser, even if the dog sat in the back seat behind the grille. He drove us through the throng of reporters and they ran at the car and yelled questions at me. Anubis also declined to comment.

Roy took the long way around to Anna's house to shake news vans that might be following. There weren't any. We toured the side streets and retraced a portion of our route before turning down Anna's block, where I could still hear them beyond the brush. I felt like we were picking up ransom money. We pulled over to the curb and he said, "We'll do our best to keep 'em from the house, but they'll show up soon."

"Thanks for trying, Roy," I said. I left his coat and Lowell's hat on the seat.

"Why I'm here."

Anna opened the front door as the dog and I came up the ramp. Anubis ran to her like a child who'd found his mother after being lost in a department store. She patted his thick forehead. It was clear to me that she wanted to get into a deep discussion. I did not want to talk. The phone had already been unplugged.

She broke into a humorless smile, one composed of consolation and tinged with a private joke, as if only she and I understood a particular family saga or curse. "Of course you know I heard what happened, Jonathan."

She often made statements pertaining to what I knew. I only wished I knew everything she said I did, or that knowing it was ever a matter of course.

"What did they say on the news?" I asked.

Her hair shined as she moved past the front window; the setting sun giving her a vermillion aura. "Nothing really, mere speculation and promises to keep their viewers further updated as the story continued to unfold. Channel thirty-five mentioned your name and held 'interviews' with bystanders, who were mostly children and teenagers. They gave accounts of playing with Anubis, witnessing your struggle in the park, and its grim ending. Several vulgar youths first described and then graphically portrayed your attacker's death throes." She sneered. "Garish little beasts."

"Cripes," I said.

"And because of your involvement, interest in the DeGrase case has resurfaced, and retrospectives are planned. The story has also broken in New York City. Debi called twice, 'Boss.' She is extremely worried."

"All this in a couple of hours."

"The media is nothing if not prompt," Anna said, "and intrusive. They'll be here soon, no doubt."

"And we still don't know anything."

Cleaning the dog got first priority. I couldn't stand the smell much longer. I lifted Anubis and stuck him in the bathtub, soaped and washed him down hastily and soaped him again, taking my time scrubbing out the deep filth. Blood and dirt streamed into the drain; he worked his mouth as if trying to spit up the taste of a dead man, or else he was just getting hungry. Anna wheeled herself in behind me and said, "You

should not mask your feelings, dear. I believe I understand what's on your mind."

"Really," I said.

"Yes," she said.

"Then you know why I prefer to mask my
feelings."

"I do." The thin rubber tires squeaked on
the tile floor. She had a book rack beside the
toilet, filled with first editions and rarities I
could've made a mint on at the store. How
she kept them in such good condition in the
bathroom, I couldn't guess. "But I fervently
wish it were not so. You did not kill that
man."

Anubis sniffed at the bubbles and
sneezed. He stood ready to shake off and I
forced him back into the water. "Tech-
nically speaking, no, I didn't."

She was not in the mood to converse, but
rather to dictate. "You did not cause this."

"The guy said differently." I shifted on the
edge of the tub and threw handfuls of warm
water over the dog's back. "He said I made it
happen by being nosy. He told me it —
whatever *it* was — was an accident."

"Richie's death?"

"Or leaving him in your trash," I said. "Or
Margaret dying. Or Karen's involvement. I
wonder which?"

"I do not believe that all these answers

an be found in a note that the sheriff may r may not have received and be hiding."

"It's a good starting place. Did you speak o him this afternoon?"

"Yes," Anna said, slightly frustrated, aught between two topics. She let out a reath in a gentle whistle that jerked the log's head up; maybe he thought she vanted him to tear somebody else's throat ut.

Picking up her original train of thought, he said, "You are not accountable. You cerainly did not invite him to ambush you, onathan."

"No."

My grandmother did not mean to be relundant or to keep at me; it was the way it appened, at times like these, when she was vorried and her exterior softened and I put up a wall or two around my usually sensitive elf. We temporarily traded positions, which nade us both equally uncomfortable. We vould work through it quickly, but not quite ast enough to completely suit either of us. You did not force him to attempt to kill ou."

"That's true," I said. "However, something did. We touched a nerve."

"Thus spurring him to action. He came lear from the shadows because he was frightened. Why? What prompted his attack? If he was afraid of exposure, why would he so clumsily expose himself? What can you recall about him, his manner, his characteristics?"

"Just his haircut," I said. "And hostility. He knew how to use a knife. He had a terrible calm in his eyes."

"Anger directed solely at you, as if you had somehow upset his scheme."

"I guess." My thoughts kept turning back to when he had asked, *Why didn't you stay out of it?* He'd almost been pleading. "It was like he was just throwing a temper tantrum. He was vicious. Demented, maybe, but I don't really think he wanted to kill me so much as he wanted me out of the way, and was willing to kill me to do it."

"He was fueled by venom," she said.

"More like he was a brat. He seemed to take my interference personally, but only so far as he had to get past me before he could go on to something else. He must have thought I knew more about him than I did."

"Then we can assume he had a specific goal he had not yet achieved. The deaths of Margaret, Karen and Richie were means to an end."

"To what? And was he working alone?"

"I would hazard to guess no," she said.

"So would I. He was probably dropped off at the park, and, considering how fast he got out of Raimi's the other night, he had somebody waiting for him in the parking lot. Nobody could remember serving him. He walked right in, saw me, grabbed a bottle off some table and picked a fight to put me out of the game."

"Whatever he was doing, I do not think it was a game."

"Whatever he was doing," I said, "he didn't think he'd be staring at the ceiling of the morgue tonight with most of his face gone."

Anna handed me a towel and I dried Anubis. He was ready to go back and finish our run in the park, the incident placed aside. He went to the front door and thumped a paw, and looked mildly irritated when I did not open it for him. Anna wheeled herself near the reading table. After a moment, Anubis resolved himself and lay down behind her.

"Thank you for attempting to salve my conscience, Anna," I said, "but I don't need any. It's not easy watching a man — even one who is trying to kill me — die in front of my eyes. I don't feel guilty. If the dog hadn't come along, I would have stabbed that bastard through his heart. I was ready to do that. I think most people would have been." She stared and slowly blinked twice. "I'm going to take a shower."

"Yes, dear," she said softly.

I went upstairs to my room and got clean clothes, stripped off the cruddy sweats and got under the hot spray. I was out in two minutes. I didn't feel that dirty or chilly. In fact, I felt pretty good. When I returned to the living room, Anna was putting *The French Powder Mystery* back onto the shelf and was taking down Ed Gorman's *Blood Moon*.

I laid out on the couch with my legs on the pillows. I felt some strain in my calves, my chest hurt, and crew cut had gotten some more jabs into my gut. "What did Broghin have to say?" I asked.

She sniffed. "First I went to his office, where I learned he was off duty, so I continued to his home. We spoke for less than half an hour before the call came which took him to the park."

"I always remember Broghin being at the station, all the time, but apparently he's been taking a lot of time off."

"Yes," she said.

"Did you ask him about the letter?"

"No," she said.

"Wasn't quite as easy as you thought it would be."

Anna continued to hold *Blood Moon* in her hands, noticed and put it down on the table. "Well, I couldn't bring it up in polite conversation while sitting with Clarice. She's taken up baking as of late. A hobby, really, to help pass the time. If her cheesecake is any portent I'd say she's better off inclined towards other recreational avenues. Masonry, perhaps."

"Another wash-out."

"Not entirely," she said. "I did notice the house was recently repainted."

Nobody paints in February, when snowstorms raged around every corner.

Anna's gaze became very sharp. "I think someone must have scrawled obscenities and he has spent time eliminating them."

"Any idea what they were?"

"None."

"That sounds as if they're being harassed," I said. "So why isn't he talking? Getting the rest of the force involved?"

"Clarice was extremely agitated. Still, I must confront either her or Franklin with pertinent questions. While avoiding further servings of cheesecake."

"I'll have to do this the hard way. Sneak into Broghin's office and snatch the note, if the damn thing even exists."

"That is not wise, Jonathan," she said,

which I knew was not the same thing as her telling me not to do it. "Don't you have a date tonight?" she asked.

I checked my watch. It was already after six.

"Oh shit," I said.

I had no idea how long Broghin would be tied up at the park, or whether he'd go straight home afterwards — I thought he would — but either way I had to see Katie before anything else. Breaking our first date did not bode well for continued romantic liaisons. Meeting her had been the only good circumstance of my return, and I didn't want to give her up.

Prairie Lane was a circular street that led to The Orchard Inn, a sort of boarding house. It had ten or fifteen rooms run by Mr. and Mrs. Leone, an elderly Italian couple who used to always tip well and feed me Florentine recipes when I was their paper boy. I walked in and Mr. Leone greeted me in his customary manner; he was a big man who liked to give bear-hugs. I tightened my muscles and tried to keep my ribs from being crushed. He went so far as to pinch my cheeks before giving me Katie's room number.

It was at the rear of the second floor. I

knocked and waited half a minute before Katie opened the door, smiling. She wore a snug, strapless black dress that ended a mile and a half above her knees. Her earrings matched her eyes. I wondered how big a puddle a man of my size would make if he spontaneously combusted in the hallway.

Katie gave me the once over, frowned, and said, "I think I may have overdressed."

"You're perfect," I said. "And it also proves you're not a big TV watcher."

"Not today, anyway. I spent the past couple of hours making myself beautiful."

"You have achieved your purpose."

"Now that you know my secret, have I broken the spell?"

"It has been duly reinforced."

"You say the sweetest things, but I have the feeling I'm getting the brush off."

"Not exactly," I said.

She went, "Hmmm," and drew a fingernail along her lower lip. I began to realize what I was giving up to go steal a letter from the sheriff who would then throw me back into jail. I began to realize I was a pretty stupid person.

"Don't mind the boxes," she said. "I've been unpacking for weeks, but I keep buying junk so it's a never ending battle to find spots for everything. I know the place is small, but I like it."

"It's bigger than my apartment."

She walked to the sofa and motioned me beside her. I sat and couldn't quite manage to free myself from her eyes. "So what are we doing here, Jonathan?"

I gave her an edited report on the events of the afternoon and told her why I had to break our date — nothing sounded especially dramatic when you laid it so simply on the line — Anubis killing a man came across like a scene from a Disney movie, as if we'd all just been playing in the snow. Katie's face filled with concern, warmth, and real fear. She slid over and held me and seemed to understand volumes about what I never could have told her anyway. Her intuition led her to whisper all the right things. We kissed and I drew her to me and pressed against her, the moment lengthening as the kiss grew more intense, and she wrapped her arms around me and the raw flash of pain lit up my head.

"What?" she said.

"Nothing."

"Is it your chest again?" She took the edge of my shirt and lifted it in the same way Wallace had. Her hands were skillful and cool. "This might seem a little barbaric," she said, "but I can fix this up for you here and now with my first aid kit. If you wait much longer it might turn septic and become a rather awful scar."

"Okay."

She dug for her kit in four different places before finally finding it at the bottom of a large box which also contained pillows, magazines, tablecloths, magic markers, dishes, aspirin, candles, and everything else this side of Atlantis.

"If I'd cut myself shaving I would have bled to death by now," I said.

"Bitch, bitch, bitch," she said. She took the kit into the bathroom and ran water and opened and shut the medicine cabinet. She returned with a couple of bottles and her jaw set firmly. "Sit on the sofa and stare straight ahead. It will only take a minute. Don't look while I do this."

"Exactly what are you going to do?" I asked.

"If I told you, Jon, it would be as bad as if you were looking."

Whatever she did, it hurt like hell, but at the same time there was a certain sexual electricity in her touch. Her fingers moved gracefully and tickled when I wasn't cringing. She cleaned the wound and gave me a glass of ice water and then we made out for a few minutes. There came a point

233

when I knew I would either leave right then or I'd lose any chance of getting out of there.

"I have to go," I said.

Katie nodded and smiled. She took off her earrings and threw them onto the coffee table. "Hell of a first date," she said and gave me a last peck. "I hope I don't have to visit you in the hospital for our second one."

I passed two news vans as they headed back for the turnpike. The parking lot of the police station was empty; inside, the boiler remained broken and precipitation ran down the open windows. Meg was at her desk, packing things into her purse and getting ready to leave. Roy and two other deputies were deep in hushed conversation. They glanced up without stopping and gave me curt nods. I passed by quickly, hoping cops couldn't really sense criminal activities in their guts as many of them suggested.

Lowell was in his office, leaning back in his seat, looking out the window again, a spire of paperwork on his filing cabinet ready to topple onto his shoulders. I snuck by without quite getting onto my tippy-toes. Broghin's door stood open and the room was empty. I went in and left the door a few inches ajar, shadows looming. I recalled

Robert Wagner from *It Takes a Thief*, and thought that being a cat burglar wasn't so difficult. Broghin's desk was from another age, two hundred pounds of squatting mahogany with gouges and burns. I opened drawers and rummaged through them, and it didn't take me long to find the note. He hadn't bothered to hide it; the letter proved to be yellowed and crinkled from the years, and the hands, and snow which had fallen on it while covering Richie Harraday's leg.

The windows in the sheriff's office were closed. Sweat dripped into my eyes as I read the letter that Lowell had said was a love note from Broghin's wife, Clarice.

I sat in the sheriff's seat and carefully went through the letter again; it was only one side of a page, three lengthy paragraphs written in a diminutive script. I didn't learn much more on the second reading; Lowell had been right, it was what you would consider your basic love letter, full of lots of emoting and weak metaphors and garden imagery — but there was a nuance beyond that, something out of kilter, maybe a little obsessive.

I got up and walked into Lowell's office and tossed the letter in his lap. He picked it up and said, "Even when you have no slack at all you find a way to hang yourself."

"It's unsigned," I said. "And there's no salutation."

His eyes narrowed as he stood. Even his hair looked muscular and irate. He took a breath and his chest expanded to an incredible degree, and I had no doubt he could pick me up with one hand and launch me through the window if he wanted to. Actually, it was clear he wanted to, I just hoped he didn't choose to.

"Why do you keep putting pressure on when it'll get you nowhere?" he asked.

"Look at the note," I said. "There's something weird."

"What?"

"Read it."

"No, I've had enough of your game."

"Read the goddamn thing. Don't skim this time." His face hardened and flushed. Strong as he was, he'd never make it on the NYPD. There was a line of probity he wouldn't cross, and on occasion that held him back from getting to the bottom of things. "Look at the style. The tilt of the handwriting."

Lowell finally read it through carefully, taking his time. He folded his arms. "Yeah."

"A man wrote this. It's not to Broghin from his wife."

"You're right," he admitted.

236

"So did he write it?"

"No, not his script." Roy walked in and Lowell shot him a look and Roy turned around and left. "I don't know if you're crazy or if this means something. If it doesn't I'm going to hand you your head. But I'm willing to talk to him."

Lowell snatched the phone and called the sheriff at home. He spoke politely, without intimation of what we'd been discussing. At one point, he rolled his eyes. He hung up and said, "I should've known. Your grandmother's over there. You shoot high and she shoots low. You two are like tag team mud wrestlers."

We sat staring into space for fifteen minutes, the heat of the office making it hard to breathe even with the windows open, and then Broghin walked in. He saw the letter on the desk and his eyes clouded. He looked far off at a point somewhere between Lowell and me and whispered, "Who the hell do you think you are?" He was already covered in sweat, droplets plinking off the end of his nose. "You went into my desk, through my stuff, as if . . . as if . . ." He couldn't come up with anything more than that, but maybe he wanted to say *as if you had the right*. I felt angry and apologetic, and I still didn't know if the love letter meant anything.

I said, "The note was left on Richie's body." He was silent, staring. "You took it off him. Why?"

"Get out of here," he said.

"Who wrote it?"

"I said —"

"Why was it left behind?"

He jabbed his meaty fingers into my chest and pain erupted. "I'm sheriff of Felicity Grove. I am the law. You don't order me around, boy." He shoved me backward and poked harder in the same spot and blue stars flared at the edges of my vision. "You don't steal from me." I held up my hands and he swatted them away and kept jabbing. The room got smaller and the heat was like the pressure of an ocean on top of us. "You don't ride me." Jab. We both looked at the desk chair at the same time. "You don't even think about getting in my face, boy, 'cause I'll bury you under the jail house." He shoved me again and pressed me back to the wall, and then came at me once more. I blocked him and turned and he swung on me, his stomach bouncing as if he'd eaten three belly dancers. I ducked and punched him in the stomach — there was really no place else you could hit him — and then we were into it. His meaty right fist caught me on the jaw and I hit him in the nose, and he drew his gun. He pointed it at my face and Lowell got in front of me the same way he had protected Aaron Bubrick.

Roy ran in and said, "Jesus Christ, sheriff, Lowell." He didn't know what to do and fumbled at his gun belt. "Jesus Christ."

Broghin bled from where he'd bitten into his lip. Flowing pink swirled along the sweat trails down his chin. "You'll get more than three months this time," he said. The gun was still pointed at Lowell's heart.

Time is relative, so perhaps we all didn't remain like that for the hour it felt like. Broghin's shirt was drenched, his face swimming. Roy's head bobbed back and forth between me and the sheriff as if he was watching tennis. Only Lowell remained calm. Another deputy ran in, and my hopes of making a timely escape continued to dwindle. He wet his lips, eyes on the gun, and quietly said, "It's your wife, sheriff, she says somebody's trying to break into the house."

"My Christ," Broghin groaned. He scowled at Lowell and holstered the gun, backing out of the room. "Get everybody over there now."

Lowell was on the move after him down the hall. I sprinted with them and said, "I'm coming."

"No," Lowell told me. He grabbed me by

the collar and stopped me solid. "Meg's gone home." Roy and the other deputy were already out the front door. The phone receiver was lying up on Meg's desk. "You stay on the line with them."

"But . . ."

"Do as you're told, damn it." In one fluid motion he grabbed a rifle from the rack and ran out.

I picked up the phone.

13

"Mrs. Broghin?"

"Who is this?" she breathed. Her voice was strained and hushed. "Lowell?"

"Jonathan Kendrick."

She let out a brief moan, clipped and quiet. "Johnny, where is my husband?"

"He's on his way." I sounded as ineffectual as I felt. My heart hammered, sand and salt formed at the edges of my eyes, and the windows were steamed over.

"Thank God," she said.

"Are you all right? Is my grandmother okay?"

"Yes, yes, we're fine." The wheelchair squeaked loudly behind her whispers.

Clarice wasn't listening. I heard the phone crackle against her blouse as she clutched it to her and turned, distracted, and I could imagine her looking out the windows at the foliage out front, the partition of maples, and the dark road beyond. A century ago the Broghin house had been a farm with several hundred acres, but each succeeding generation had sold off more of the land until it was now surrounded by less than three or four square acres. It was laid back at the rim of western dale, not fifteen minutes from the station, but secluded from neighbors nonetheless.

"Is there a gun in the house?" I asked.

Her murmuring proved awful to hear, fright cutting her voice into a staccato of gasps. "Frank's got a dozen of them, but they're all locked up in his cabinet and I have no idea where the keys are."

"Look for them. Put Anna on."

"The lights are dead." There was a disturbing sound in the background I couldn't make out. *"Why is it saying that?"*

"What?" This was the worst, I thought, unable to help or move or do anything but listen.

"There's somebody out there," she whimpered.

"Put Anna on."

"No!" she cried. "Don't you understand? I've never held anything so tightly before as this phone. Don't leave us."

"The police are on their way. They'll be there in a couple of minutes. You'll be all right. Let me speak with my grandmother."

The noise grew louder and Anna was talking, tone smooth and endearing as if she were speaking to a child. Clarice said, "Why does it keep saying that?" She began crying, husky, desperate weeping that consumed her, to the point where I thought she'd hyperventilate. There was another rustling of the receiver pressed against her, distant rumblings of a crude ethereal voice, and complaints and sobs as Anna struggled to take the phone and comfort her.

"Hello, Jonathan," Anna said. "Excuse my presumptions, but I somehow expected you to lead the cavalry."

"I'm supposed to be keeping you rational. What the hell is happening there?"

"It is lovely to hear your voice," she said, "and I'm glad I have the chance to speak with you. We were talking when the lights went out. Strange that the phone is still working, since they had taken the time to tamper with the power lines."

Sweat poured down my neck, landing with patters, and my mouth went dry. She acted as if we were telephoning to exchange household hints on the best ways to remove lipstick stains; I think I'm the only one in the world who could hear the diffidence beneath her controlled exterior. "Who is it? What are they saying?"

As always, she focused on the situation at hand. "I cannot be certain if it is a man or a woman. I believe it is a modified tape recording. Weird intonations keep repeating, 'You deserve your death, you've earned it.' The wind has risen and makes it even more difficult to distinguish." She held the phone out so I could listen, but the sounds were too indistinct. "There is more, but the voice is garbled, keening, almost subhuman. Doubtlessly, it was intended to have just the effect it's had on Clarice." She paused and said something reassuring to Broghin's wife, and I could hear Clarice speaking. Anna relayed it to me. "Over the past several nights they have been vexed with other forms of harassment as well."

"Since Richie's death."

"Yes, and we were correct in our assumption that obscenities were painted on the house. It read Love Kills. Rather trite, I'd say. There were also distressing phone calls that Franklin insisted Clarice not mention to anyone."

"More of his secrets."

"Foolish man." The keening faded as she spoke. "Wait. The voice has stopped." I could hear the phone cord snapping and untangling as she wheeled herself along. "Although the outside lights are out, too, the moon on the snow provides adequate lighting. I don't see anyone. An engine is turning over in the distance, at the bottom of the drive, I think. They're leaving. We're fine, Jonathan, don't worry."

She was doing a better job of reassuring herself than I was. "I should be there."

She said, "You are here."

Clarice gargled out nervous laughter.

Anna laughed, too, quite solemnly and briefly. "The sirens are nearby." Another two minutes or so passed. "Yes, here are the police cruisers pulling up now." The play-by-play further ostracized me from the moment, alone and safe in the police station while my grandmother was being hounded and threatened by a killer I was still no closer to catching. Failure upon failure, piled one on the other to attest to my lack of insight. "Now Franklin, Deputy Tully, and several other deputies are outside, poised and ready. The direct approach. I do hope they don't start firing at shadows." She tsked them. She tsked them, but not me.

Broghin's voice was high and scared as he came through the front door. Clarice's cries of relief and slurpy kisses for her husband filled the line.

"Quite an exuberant reunion," Anna said. She lowered her voice. "Such a silly woman, really, one would think a sheriff's wife would have a bit more self-control. Hmmm, how odd. It appears that willow swatches

245

have been left lying against the door. What a strange perpetrator."

Then Broghin, Lowell, and Anna were talking, and Clarice kept laughing and weeping. Roy said, "All clear around back," and somebody hung up the phone.

I ran a light and lost control on a slick patch, jumped the curb and took out a mail box on Wisteria Way. The Jeep's bumper hooked a fire hydrant and broke off without argument, left skittering down the road. I nearly overturned before I got to the cemetery.

Winds blew the new snowfall in intricate layers strung across the tombstones. Moonlight reflected off the entire yard. Ice and stone sculptures rose against the backdrop of reaching trees, standing out in the night's brightness, blue-black and silver. Felicity Grove had taken on an almost pagan atmosphere, as if praying madonnas and reverent angels now worshipped Diana, goddess of the moon. Low-hanging branches scooped channels in the snow, and wood clacked solidly against wood. Crummler's shack was dark and lifeless. I banged on the door. There was no movement inside. I banged again.

From directly behind the doorknob, near the floor as if he had dropped to his knees, Crummler said, "Leave me alone!"

"It's Jonathan Kendrick."

"Oh."

Zebediah Crummler opened the door an inch and peered out; his eyes were as wild as ever, but the happy, manic energy had vanished. He clutched a tattered Bible to his chest, rocking it the way a child hugs a doll. His beard was threaded with barbs and splashes of sap. When he saw me he smiled and dropped the Bible, began snapping his fingers, shivering, fidgeting. "I am here, Jon!"

"I need to talk to you."

"My shoes have some mud on them now, but not too much." He ducked back inside, turned on a light, and brought me his shoes. "Do you see?"

"That's good," I said.

"Yes, I don't want you to get mad."

"I wouldn't be mad," I said. The wind blew hard against my back where my sweaty shirt was now freezing. I stepped around him and he shut the door and picked up the worn Bible. "I understand how hard it is to keep them clean when you work so hard to keep this place nice."

He shuddered, gyrated his hips, tapped his foot rapidly. "I like doing it."

"Did I scare you?" I asked.

"Yes," he said, grinning.

"I need you to take me to Potter's Field."

The smile stayed nailed to his face but his eyes dimmed. "I don't like it there."

"I know you don't," I said, "but I need your help."

"You need Crummler's help?" he asked.

"To fight the forces of darkness," I said.

"From a interdimensional cosmos where the wraiths of gigantic demons seek possession of our very astral plane?"

"Yes."

"I will help you!"

"Tell me about the ghost," I said.

He wrapped his arms more tightly around his shoes and the Bible. "I don't want to."

Terror and ignorance walked hand-in-hand around this town unchecked, taking turns frightening elderly ladies and haunting the dim-witted innocent. Crew cut and his partner *were* playing games: teasing, heckling, badgering. I grabbed Crummler's shoulders and gaped at him in awe. "You?" I said. "Frightened? But you are Crummler! Hero of the unfortunate, saver of worlds. There is no one else I can turn to at this desperate time." It perked him up, and he started jitterbugging. "You have returned from battles with the dark corridors of far-off dimensions."

"Yes, yes," he said. "A war that has raged

for eons in each of the infinite macrocosms; the deaths of fragile stars shine down on us. The forces of evil are forever being marshalled, chaos seeks to firmly establish a toe-hold on the Earth, but I will not fail in my efforts for I am Crummler!"

"Tell me about the ghost," I said, "who chases you with the willow swatches."

"My foe." He edged sideways to a wooden chair and sat heavily. "It was here tonight. I thought you were it, coming to chase and hit and yell bad things at me. It bangs on the windows sometimes."

"What does it look like?" I asked.

"It comes when it is cold."

"But what does it look like?"

"When it is cold, its face is covered. Bundled. Black and red. Scarves."

"You've got to be kidding me."

"I kid you not, Jon."

"A man or a woman?"

"A demon."

Crap: I'd pressed him too far into his own mythos. He happily stared at me, put his hands up to his face and waved. You have to take everything in order, deal with exactly what you have at the moment. Somehow, you must control your impatience and take each separate event and coax them until they fit.

"Okay," I said. "Take me to the Field."

"It's too dark."

"The moon on the snow makes it bright outside."

"All right, Jon." He placed the Bible on his chair and put on his shoes. They were still laced, and he had to shove and grind and coerce his feet into them. He whirled his dirty coat around himself like a cloak, and we walked south to Potter's Field.

Crummler had done the work of an entire Boy Scout troop in the two days since I'd last been here. No wonder he looked such a mess; the amount of effort it took was amazing. The underbrush had been cut down and smoothed back. Grappling, diseased trees had been pruned. He'd hacked away at the confines of the landscape, clearing the grade, digging up ancient stumps from the frozen earth. Fallen headstones had been righted, and he'd carefully piled the broken bits of those that had crumbled into gravel. Meticulously, Crummler had even cleaned out the worn, carved numbers of identification.

And he had taken pains to arrange the willow swatches in a decorous fashion on that particular marker.

"I keep the Field clean now," he said. "That is why there is some mud on my shoes. But not too much."

I bent and examined the area. "Who's buried here?"

"The ghost of a ghost." Crummler liked that and smiled pleasantly. "The chance of a ghost. The father of ghosts." He stooped and carefully realigned the swatches I had knocked out of position. "Nobody. Only had a pauper's funeral."

"You sound as if you know who he was. Do you know his name?"

"No, they have no names," he said. "It's better to let them stay buried."

"Yes, you've told me."

He pointed at nearby graves. "Here is Louise May Murphy's abortion. Twelve years ago, no name. And there's the hitch-hiker who died outside town, hit and run. No name. And over there is . . ."

"And here?" I asked.

"The man the sheriff shot."

"Broghin killed this man?"

Nodding, he swooped closer. "Know you not, Jon?" He was surprised it had taken me this long to only get it to half-speed. "A long time ago, it was. Maybe twenty-five or thirty years ago, but I remember. He wasn't sheriff then, and did not have a big fat belly. The mayor made a speech and gave him a medal. Then the sheriff who wasn't the sheriff yet made a speech and there was a parade and the people bought lemonade on the corner. I only listened for a while and then I had to go to the hospital and then come here to rake."

"Why did Broghin kill the man?" I asked.

"He was a bad man."

"But what did he do?"

Crummler mimed handing me gifts. "He came from the blackness and left things for the women. Nice things, I think, sweet things, things I wish someone had brought me back in the hospital. Three of them. Three women, three presents. It went on for a long time, they said. Candy and letters. That was not the bad part. I heard people laughing about it. It was a lot of fun, they said." A single large shudder passed through him from head to toe as if somebody had wrung him out like a wet towel. "Then they found two of the ladies dead. The last was saved by the sheriff who was not the sheriff yet, who killed the villain." He turned and the moon caught the energy in his eyes. "The flower lady," he said.

Margaret Gallagher had been stalked twenty-five years ago.

"And now the ghost comes here at night," he sighed. "To yell at me for not taking good care of the Field. And sometimes it brings the baby."

"The baby."

Crewcut's face flashed the same way as his knife, and other faces came into focus too; the scrawled script of a letter written in a dangerously romantic tone, pieces pulling together like film of a mirror breaking, running backwards, reforming.

And those words: *How could it mean anything?*

The unplowed back trails made driving difficult, but I kept to the twin grooves cut in the deep snow by other trucks before me. The tires of the Jeep threatened to get stuck twice, but I kept the speed at a constant forty and managed to buck free both times.

The houses east of Warner Fork looked like they'd been cut from crystal. Spray from the river added extra layers of ice to the eucalyptus and pine. I slowed and parked up close to the house. The river raged, chops louder than earlier in the week, wind playing eerie pipes of Pan all along the length of the woods. Flickering lights of a television and receding smoke from the fireplace proved somebody was home. I got out and quickly crossed the yard. The motorcycle leaned up against the side of the house. I checked the engine. It was warm. I thought the recent snowfall would have kept everybody to cars, but I suppose bikers don't mind being out in any kind of weather.

I knocked on the door and had a long wait. Drapes rustled at the window. Deena finally appeared. At her side, Fred and Barney stuck their noses out, black shale eyes fixed.

Deena had expression this time; red and toxic hatred swarmed her face, those mismatched lips immediately tugging and crawling as if the dogs' command to kill kept passing half-formed over her tongue. Her eyes remained uncannily calm. We were close. I couldn't quite be sure if I was smiling. The sexual charge had become ever more powerful.

"Hello," I said.

The breeze tugged her scarlet hair across her face, obscuring that weird mouth. She breathed softly, "What?" She didn't sound like she was asking me what I wanted but rather what was going to happen next. I wondered.

"I need to speak with Tons for a minute."

"No." The word fell like a stone.

My voice grew almost as tight as hers. "It's extremely important."

"He's asleep."

"He does a lot of that."

Her bottom lip curled, really *curling*

twisting and rearing ugly the way the Wicked Witch of the East's feet curled under the house Dorothy dropped on her. "What?"

"Please," I said, trying to keep it together and feeling my tolerance slipping off me like dead skin. "I know I've been something of a bother the past couple of days, but I need to speak with him."

"No."

She went to shut the door and I jammed my foot inside, got a position on the jamb and shoved. *Dogs,* I thought, *be careful of the dogs.* The front door flew open and blasted back against the wall. The Dobermans had been ready to get into me for days; they darted forward, keyed up yet silent. If dogs really could smell fear then they weren't getting much of a noseful off me. Instead they looked surprised, catching the lingering scents of crew cut's blood. Fred came low and Barney hit high, one tearing at my ankle and the other standing on his hind legs and going for my throat. If I hadn't seen Anubis in action I wouldn't have known what to do. What irony if I died the same way. Deena vanished. I caught Barney's collar as he snapped at my neck and tugged him up and over my shoulder and hurled him out the storm door, which smashed and went flying on impact. Fred had already started chomping at my leg. His snout was dabbed with two thin streaks of my blood. I brought both fists down heavily on top of his skull. The dog let out a yelp and slumped to the ground, and I grabbed him by the collar and flung him on top of his brother. I slammed the door shut.

A baby cried in the far room. I stepped cautiously into the kitchen, checking, then walked into the living room. Tons was sprawled out and sleeping on the couch, undisturbed by the commotion. One arm was flung over his face and the other rested on the floor near another empty bottle of JD. I moved into Richie's room, where Deena was loading the Winchester.

She spun and pointed the rifle at me, but she hadn't locked the barrel. I said, "You shouldn't have wasted time loading so many bullets," and took the Winchester from her and laid it on the bed behind me.

"You," she said. "What do you think you're doing?"

"Saving my life, probably."

The baby still cried. Deena slung that emotionless gaze as she slid past and went into the baby's room across the hall and picked up her daughter. The room was filled with the usual amount of stuffed animals, toys and clothes she wouldn't be able to apreciate for another year or two. Deena rocked and shushed her daughter. The infant sat wrapped in a large, black and red wool blanket, and Deena buried her face in the cloth as she hummed to the baby. The scene would have done Norman Rockwell proud, if only there wasn't such a hideous underside to it.

"You keep ol' Maurice on a shorter leash than you do your dogs," I said. "Whenever you want to go out alone or keep him home, you hand him a bottle and a handful of downers and he puts himself to sleep."

"You were stupid to come alone," she said.

I tried imagining her with that fun scarlet mane buzzed off. "Not only do you act like him but you sound like him, too." She wasn't going to attempt lying her way out of anything; she didn't have the temperament or theatrics. "That is who the guy with the crew cut was, wasn't it? Your brother?"

"You murdered him."

"Not exactly."

Her hair jounced like crashing waves and turned me on even more. How that kind of sexual quality had led her to Tons Harraday I'd never know, but it blasted out at me in a torrent of rage and sorrow. "I'll kill you for that."

"He was staying here in the back trailer."

"For that." Deena repeated herself, stuck in the moment as she pressed her face to the infant again. "For that."

"You were doing it to her as well, weren' you? Harassing Margaret Gallagher, the way your father had twenty-five years ago. Why?" It had taken time to deciphe Crummler's monologue. He'd said the ghost of a ghost, the chance of a ghost, the father of ghosts. "How long had it been going on? How long did you hound tha woman before she finally died of a heart at tack?"

"Not enough. Not at all. It wasn't lik that," Deena said. "I just wanted to talk to her. You don't understand. I tried talking to her on the phone, I wanted to see her, to know what my father felt, and why. I jus wanted to look at her, I wanted to know wh she" — again the curling lip, and the tide o hatred rushing up, making speech difficul — "broke my father's heart. I never knev him, but he loved her; I think he loved her The letters he wrote, they were beautiful He deserved a proper burial. They shoul have done that for him. I wanted to talk bu she kept hanging up on me."

Here I'd been wallowing in my own pas believing myself haunted in some way: jus

look into those eyes, deader than her dogs'
— what had driven her and her brother to
Felicity Grove after twenty-five years to
complete a madman's insane agenda? Dis-
placed, I thought, all that fury. I should've
been listening more closely to my grandmother. Anna had called it venom. Deena's
face, body language, every nuance was an-
gled wrong as if she'd been crushed and tied
up again with chicken wire.

"Why did you wait so long? You were
living in town for almost a year."

"Because, you damn fool . . ." Her breath
came in gasps; there'd be no logic to this. Insanity might've been learned or genetic, but
whatever its cause, she'd caught it good.
Stray tears of fury dripped and clung halfway down her cheeks. "Because I didn't
know that this was the damn town. I'm from
Gallows, about a hundred miles west of
here. I met Tons and I loved him, and I
didn't know. My mother died two months
ago and my brother Carl found a carton
filled with our father's belongings: some of
the letters he never sent, and newspaper ar-
ticles. Mother clipped and pasted them on
black cardboard just like school pictures.
She knew what he was, and how he'd been
killed, but never told anyone, and let them
bury him without a name. It didn't matter

that we didn't know where he was really buried; they all could have been him. We simply picked a site. Where that filthy, idiot gravekeeper let the weeds cover my daddy — that retard's lucky Carl didn't break his neck. That's how I learned about why my father left when we were only three and four years old. Who he was, what he did, and how he died."

"And Carl came here and you both started making calls to Margaret?"

"Only me. Carl couldn't do anything but think about the day when Daddy left and never came back. Carl found out the cop who killed our daddy was the sheriff now and started calling him too, and sending presents the way the papers said our daddy had done. Carl thought it was poetic justice. I did, too. Tons didn't know."

"What do the willow swatches mean?"

She actually smiled and I wished she hadn't. "It was Carl's idea. He left them because our house in Gallows had a large willow tree out back and our daddy built us a treehouse in it. Nothing big, just a few planks nailed together, but the three of us always played there. It fell apart but Daddy rebuilt it, until he didn't come home any-more."

My mouth was dry; there wasn't enough

satisfaction in this, not the way I'd hoped. "And Richie?"

Deena cocked an ear and I heard the sound too: Tons snoring, muttering, smacking his lips, and one of the dogs growling at the door. It shook her as she repeated what she'd said the other day, with the same empty tone. "He was a good kid." The baby had hushed and Deena whispered. "But he was silly and stupid. He thought we were doing it for fun, like a game. I still just wanted to see her, but she wouldn't even open the door. We were scared she'd call the police. Richie broke in through the back and let me and Carl in. She started to scream and Carl shoved her and then shoved her again, yelling about our father, and Richie started getting scared. I grabbed her and shook her and she slid to the floor and turned over on her back. I needed to know what my father had seen in her. I needed to know about my father, don't you understand that?" I did. "And then she was dead, just like that. Didn't take a minute." Deena's eyes glazed. "Richie thought he could make it look like a robbery and stole some jewelry, and he said he wiped his fingerprints off the glass, but he must have left some. After a few weeks he got careless and tried to pawn the bracelets and get a little cash, except he sunk himself. And . . ." She let it fade, staring at nothing.

"And your brother decided Richie was too dumb to get away clean, and when the kid got caught he'd tell the cops everything. So Carl killed Richie."

"I didn't know he would," she said, a subtle hint of pleading in her voice. It was the only time she'd shown any regret at how the circumstances had played out. More tears streaked her face down to her chin, but no sniffling, no sobbing. "They were supposed to just go driving through the park, Richie's favorite place to hang out, trying to think things through a little, and Carl said they started to argue and Richie started telling him stuff until my brother couldn't *take* Richie anymore; the kid could be like that sometimes."

Her reasoning made my hair stand on end. "So it really was a fluke that he left Richie in my yard."

"You live near the far end of the park. It must've happened right there."

"You said as much when you told me, 'How could it mean anything?' It just happened to be a nice spot for his impromptu act of leaving one of your father's old letters for Broghin. And tonight you watched his house. You found my grandmother there and saw Broghin leave and then you set up your little Wizard of Oz skit." All a game, so very fun. "Why didn't you cut the phone wires, too?"

"I thought I did," she said. "There were a bunch of them. They were a lot thinner than I expected. I just stuck a branch behind them and pulled hard. There weren't even any sparks or anything."

"Why did you kill Karen?"

"I didn't," she said.

"Your brother, then."

"He didn't, either. There was no reason for that."

My stomach knotted. Deena walked by me and we went into the living room where Tons was still snoring in the exact same position. I kept an eye out for her trying to let the dogs back in. I picked up the phone and started to call Lowell.

Deena pulled Tons' hair until he opened his eyes and said, "What?"

She had been resigned before, but now one final chance to get out of this was still open and she gave it a shot. "He's crazy! He broke in here!" The baby began crying again. "I think he killed Richie!"

"What are you talking about?" he asked.

"He killed your brother, Tons! Get him!"

He sat up and came at me, staggering,

arms raised. I ducked his one wild punch, swung and tapped him lightly on the chin. Tons went down like his namesake's amount of bricks.

He crawled forward for a moment, pointed at my leg and said, "You're bleeding on my floor, man." I wasn't quite chastened enough to apologize for the fact. Tons tried to get up and fell asleep halfway to his knees.

Richie started telling him stuff.

The child wailed and Deena's eyes met mine.

"Is she Richie's?" I asked.

She cooed into her daughter's face, infant gripping a strand of her scarlet hair like a lifeline out of a world with such a beginning as this.

"I don't know," she said.

14

I waited until Lowell showed; he came with Roy and another deputy, both of whom had their guns drawn low for the dogs. Seeing Anubis' work earlier in the day prepared them for another encounter with savagely protective canines. But being thrown through a glass door was enough to take some of the resolve out of the Dobermans. One was semi-conscious on the porch, and the other barked insanely but wouldn't leave his brother's side.

I had told Lowell most of it over the phone and filled in the gaps when he got here. He listened without comment. The child's crying didn't distract him, and neither did Deena's humming or Tons' snoring. Roy grabbed the rifle off Richie's bed, and he and the other deputy searched the house and the trailer out back for the .22. They discovered Carl's belongings, but didn't find the gun.

At one point Lowell said, "That son of a bitch," and I knew he was talking about Broghin, who might have avoided all the trouble if only he'd leveled with his own men.

"Why do you think he didn't come clean from the beginning?" I asked.

Lowell said, "Because he was scared. Seeing that letter brought up a lot from his past. I know that story about the stalker and how Broghin tripped over him skulking around Margaret's house and killed him in a tussle, but they never found out who he was. Broghin shot the perp in the face back when he was just starting out, still the only man he ever killed. For twenty-five years he's been living with that. It does something inside."

The ghost of a ghost. The chance of a ghost.

"His own private ghost," I said. "He couldn't share it with anybody." Twenty-five years of replaying his moment up on the stage giving his speech and taking his bows.

"Yeah, I guess." Lowell looked quite ready to fold the sheriff into an origami swan. "When men like him get scared they take it on their shoulders, make it personal and muck it up. They want control, only they don't have any so they walk around with their heads half screwed off."

"I sort of told you that a few days ago."

"Yeah," he said. He'd been wrong to completely trust Broghin, and it would never be the same in town again.

"He should have given you a holler."

Deena asked if it would be all right if she changed the baby, and Roy nodded and escorted her into the other room. Tons drooled on the rug, and I didn't want to be around when they woke him up and explained what had happened. He'd lost his brother, wife, and brother-in-law, and if the police wanted to pursue the drug charges based on what they'd found in the house, he might very well not see his infant daughter for a couple of years.

Roy found the tape recorder and played it. An eerie, ghoulish keening filled the house, like a bubbling, choking victim: *"We have waited for this moment to . . ."* He shut it off quickly and muttered, "Freaky goddamn people."

Lowell motioned for me to follow him into the kitchen. I did and he turned and stared at me, granite features unreadable.

"What?" I asked.

He wet his lips and told me what Wallace had found out about Karen Bolan.

Broghin got there a few minutes later; we looked at each other for a long time while he went through the motions of taking charge of the scene. His demons had been dealt with and you could tell he felt like getting back into his old shoes. Lowell had respected him, Anna had trusted him, and his wife had loved him, and still he put them all into danger because he didn't have the strength to give up the limelit glory day of his career. He'd tampered with evidence, knew much more than he was willing to relate. He reminded me that we all had our fantasies and did our best, and occasionally acted our worst, in order to live up to them. For twenty-five years he kept a sacred memory of speeches and parades: killing Deena's father might have been the day he looked back on as the happiest of his life. He didn't want to give it up.

"Kendrick," he said. "Let me . . ."

I drew my arm back ready to haul off and break his jaw, started forward with it with all the frustration working at me like scalpels, a sudden migraine fragmenting my skull, but somewhere between me and him I lost the urge and nearly fell forward into his arms, and the room started to whirl as I looked up into his sweaty face and I had to go outside to throw up.

The worst part, perhaps, was that I meant to take time and sort the remainder through, drive around wishing for stray lightning bolts of inspiration, but instead I went immediately across town to where I understood I had to go. The subconscious mind is a perverse associate of ourselves which takes credit for our meanest assumptions; good, I thought, maybe that will help me get to sleep tonight. I didn't want to believe I had consciously thought what I was thinking. The same idea had occurred to Lowell, I was certain, but whether he held back because he was a cop and needed a warrant to do anything or because he was giving me the opportunity to end it myself, I didn't know. I hoped it was because he was a cop. This type of responsibility I could live without.

It was after eleven, but the front porch light remained on. I parked at the curb and fumbled in the back of the Jeep until I found a bent screwdriver. It would do.

I got out and started up the driveway. A cat wandered over and brushed against my leg, tail looping around my ankle. I picked her up and held her close, no longer smelling the faint antiseptic odor in her fur. She meowed loudly and nibbled at my finger. I put her down.

The door of the El Dorado was unlocked. I opened it and the hospital stink dropped on me. In the dim illumination of the dome light I could see that the weather stripping around the window was cracked and discolored in spots; I used the screwdriver to pry loose the Dezus clamps and took the door panel off. The seat, rug, and window had been cleaned, but blood and minute traces of skin tissue had run down the window seal and dried inside the car door.

Bile rose halfway up my throat, but I had nothing left to give. I got out onto the lawn and took deep breaths and thought I'd be all right, but then a second wave hit and I knew I wouldn't be. I made a dash for the primrose hedges under the mailbox and dry-heaved. I lost whatever was left in my stomach. There wasn't much, but it felt like everything I'd eaten in the past week.

In five minutes I was well enough to ring the doorbell.

Doug Hobbes answered. He looked even more distraught than his wife Lisa had been: drawn and quartered, with the meaty red bags under his eyes flaming. I couldn't even picture Karen's husband Willie looking worse than Doug did now: blank stare, patches of beard stubble and razor cut scabs, mouth like a lipstick slash. His disheveled hair spilled in ratty clumps, and I saw that his hairline had begun to recede pretty badly and he'd been covering the fact with some creative styling.

"Hello, Doug."

"Johnny," he said quietly, "come in." If he thought it was strange that I was calling at eleven-thirty at night, he didn't show it.

"Is Willie here?"

"Yes," he said, and paused. He took a step down the hall and stopped and wheeled to me again, as if he was seeing me for the first time and didn't quite remember who I was or how I got in. There wasn't much alcohol on his breath, but it wouldn't take a lot to get Doug a little high. "Uhm," he said, frowning. "Willie's upstairs sleeping in the guest room. He hasn't slept in two days, since they first called him." Doug scratched his chin too roughly and left angry lines. "His nerves are shot and he's completely exhausted."

"You could use some sleep yourself," I said.

He didn't hear me. "You know Willie can pack it away when he wants to, but he loaded himself with highballs all day and they didn't faze him. I thought he would never sleep, but about an hour ago he finally went up." Doug took a jump-start step again, stopped. "If only I'd known last night I would have flown home immediately."

Lisa came in from the living room, so

small I didn't notice her until she stood beside me. She stooped and touched my leg. "Your leg's bloody, Johnny."

"It's okay."

"I'll get a bandage."

"I'm fine. It's already stopped."

She nodded and gave Doug a concerned sidelong glance. "We heard what happened this afternoon," she said in her Tinkerbell voice. "Is there anything we can do for you?"

"A lot more's happened since then," I said.

"Oh God."

Doug tried to flatten and reshape his hair and wound up making modern art. I tried to imagine what he must be feeling and couldn't do it; you could see his thoughts running wild, numb exterior doing nothing to hide the depth of loss. "They didn't give out many details on the news. Why they call it news, I don't know, since they never seem to inform us of much. Do they have any idea why this man attacked you?"

"He killed Richie Harraday," I said.

It was reason enough for Doug; he wasn't concerned with making sense of anything. He only had need of rationalization. "The kid?" he said. "The one they found in the garbage?" Twenty different half-formed expressions slithered over his face, and for the first time he showed some life. "So you got the guy who —"

"Murdered Karen," Lisa finished.

The taste in my mouth was bad enough to gag on. Doug's capped teeth flashed brightly. "I should wake Willie," he said. "He's beat to hell, but I think he should be told as soon as possible."

"Yes," Lisa said. "Do that, honey."

He didn't move until she took him by the shoulders and led him to the stairway and gave him a small shove. "We'll be down in a couple of minutes, I guess," he said, and lurched up the steps. I had the feeling he'd pass out at the top.

The entire house still smelled disgustingly clean. Lisa got her coat from the closet and said, "Let's go outside."

"All right."

She slammed the door and the bushes erupted like a stirred hornets' nest, cats bounding over our feet. Moonglow reflected everywhere at once: off the ice, in the cats' eyes, against the hood of her shining yellow car.

"You know," she said.

I couldn't say anything.

She looked over and saw that the dome light of her Caddy was on and the passenger door had been taken apart. "I suppose that means I forgot something and you've found evidence, too." She tittered remotely. "I'm sorry."

I tried once more to speak and still couldn't. Words swam in my head but none managed to make it to my mouth. *Why?* kept darting forward like a moth attacking a candle. I could guess the answer but it seemed weak to me, proving how different we all were. I cursed Lowell and Broghin for making — for *allowing* — me to do this.

"I knew I shouldn't have dragged you into it," Lisa said. "But at the time it seemed like the smart thing to do. To put the blame on somebody else." She sat on the stoop and raised her head and gazed at me. Her tears flowed more freely than Deena's squirts of rage, streaming in thick tracks down her cheeks. "I should've known you'd catch whoever killed that boy, and that you'd realize Karen's death didn't make any sense." She hugged her belly like a chronically painful wound. "Well, aren't you going to say anything?"

I couldn't even say no.

"Damn it, Johnny."

She reached and took my hand and pulled me down to sit beside her. Like all of us, we'd known each other since grade school, through fingerpainting and puberty, first loves and last. I hoped that winning football games wouldn't be the best times I'd ever have in my life. I prayed killing Phillip Dendren wouldn't be my limelit greatest memory. Lisa could've been a cheerleader but she'd been too shy for all the yelling and dancing and crowds. It struck me how sorry I was I'd missed her wedding day.

"Damn it," she repeated.

I told her about Deena and Carl and Margaret Gallagher and the unnamed stalker. It grew difficult keeping my voice cool and even, but I did a fair job. "She claimed she and her brother had nothing to do with Karen's murder, and the police searched but never found the .22. That was one loose end. I talked to Jim Witherton and he told me Karen had been visiting Syntech a lot, bringing cookies to the guys, even when Willie wasn't around. That in itself wasn't anything much, but when I came by the other day in the middle of your cleaning jag, it seemed a little odd that you would have cleaned the car with something that smelled like industrial strength. I thought about her and Doug. And how you'd had three miscarriages." She showed no change of expression. "And Wallace discovering that Karen was pregnant." That was what had hit Doug the hardest, knowing there was at least a chance the child had been his. "Not much to go on really, but Lowell would have tripped to it eventually."

"Yes, he probably would have," she whispered, the sobs making her breaths come in awful, tiny gasps. We still held hands, and when Lisa got up she tugged me to my feet and we walked across the snowy lawn, followed by the cats. "You make it sound so nice and easy."

"No."

"They were sleeping together," she said. "Her and Doug. It's something that always happens in movies and novels, you know? The husband getting it on with the wife's best friend. It never hurts anybody in books because the two couples are so close. Everybody hops out of bed and forgives one another. Like it's a sign of maturity." She didn't say, *They were having an affair*. That would have made it sound too romantic, love on the French Riviera. "Maybe it didn't mean a great deal to you, Johnny, having the flake you had for a wife, but me . . . oh God, when I found out . . ."

She was right; it hadn't meant much to me when I learned Michelle was seeing other men, but jealousy is relative. I recalled the first moment I saw Katie, and how men passing by in the street had stopped and looked at her through the flower shop's window, and what that had done to me.

"Don't you see?" she said, bottom lip catching tears. "Don't you understand? Karen carried a child. *His* child." She dropped my hand and spun in a half circle, and the cats, as if they were her kids, went spinning along with her. "And you know what the funny part is? He couldn't stand her most of the time. He thought she was loud and stupid and obnoxious." She flung herself against my chest and cried as I tightened my arms around her. "But the baby, he needed that, and I couldn't give it to him." Before I knew it I was weeping with her, and we held each other until Doug walked out onto the porch and said furtively, "Lisa, honey? Are you all right?" Willie was behind him. The two of them with the same lost look on their faces — both lovers of a dead woman with a lovely, golden smile. Both tormented over the death of their twelve-week-old child.

15

I'd been moved out of my usual dining room seat by Katie and the sun was in my eyes. I thought about closing the curtains, but being blind gave me the advantage of not knowing whether the goop in the bowl was crawling across the table to get me. Anna put more of the gray glop on our plates and Katie said, "I'm going to explode if you feed me any more, Mrs. Kendrick."

"Please call me Anna," my grandmother said. She liked Katie a great deal, she'd told me earlier, though feeding her gray glop was not how I would have expected Anna to show affection.

"You make better goulash than my mother, and considering she's had a Czech recipe in the family for something like six generations, that's impressive."

I swirled my spoon around in the stuff and said, "Is that what this is?"

"I shall attempt to take that as a compliment, Jonathan," Anna said. "I know how food not immediately associated with hamburger tends to confuse you."

"I have bourgeois tastes," I said.

"You can't get any more bourgeois than goulash, dear."

"Okay." Maybe that was true, but this was the first time in memory when Anubis did not sit and stare steadfastly at my food while I ate. I didn't blame him.

Anna hadn't lectured or questioned me or tried to salve my conscience when I came in last night; I woke her and we sat together, and I told her everything from beginning to end. She'd listened without comment until my voice cracked. I thought I'd cried all that I could, but in the middle of it I discovered I wasn't quite finished. Afterwards, my grandmother kissed me on the forehead before I went to sleep, the way she had when I was a boy. The circle I thought I had closed when I left Felicity Grove seemed to open wider once more. This morning I'd heard her on the phone giving hell to the sheriff, and I knew there'd be more repercussions to follow. It would never be the same again, but that was fine, we'd recover from this one as we'd done in the past.

"I am going to the cemetery later this afternoon," Anna said, "if you would care to join me."

"No, I don't think so."

She nodded. "I understand. You've spent

a great deal of time there lately."

"Would you mind if I came along with you?" Katie asked. "It's been a while since I've visited Margaret's grave and I really should take some flowers."

"I would love your company."

I excused myself and went to the bathroom and when I got back they were whispering like pals in a movie theater.

"Let's go for a walk," Katie said. "It'll help digest all this good cooking."

"Cripes, you're laying it on thick."

She leaned over. "You'd better learn how it's done if you ever intend to meet my father."

"Oh boy," I said.

I didn't know if she was simply giving me the old fall-off-your-horse-get-right-back-on routine or if she really did want to go for a walk in the park. Katie called the dog and he came with a black-lipped grin on his face. We went outside and crossed the street and wound through a side path through the thicket where Carl had led Richie Harraday. Anubis sprinted off ahead of us.

"You don't seem proud of yourself," she said.

"I'm not really."

"You ought to be."

"I'm not so sure."

"I am," she said. "You did what you had to do."

"Yes, but that doesn't mean it's something to be glad about."

She stopped. "No," she said firmly. "Don't walk a line on this, Jon." I looked away and she reached and touched my chin and turned my face to her. It reinforced how much I enjoyed lovely women touching my face. "I've been watching the news. Channel thirty-five devoted an hour to your and Anna's exploits."

"Exploits," I said. That was worse than "cases."

"I've learned more about you now, and I think I know you a lot better than I did."

"And?"

"And I don't like when you kick yourself for being a brave man who does what has to be done."

"Fair enough."

We walked the short course towards the lake and stayed off the running paths. The kids weren't afraid of the dog, and he chased skaters across the ice, flopping wildly onto his side a few times. Katie said, "You're going back to the city tonight?"

"I've got an eight o'clock flight."

She went, "Hm."

"You just said a lot with that, but I need a little help with the interpretation."

"I have faith you'll eventually figure it out on your own."

"So does this count as our second date?" I asked.

"Maybe after you take me home and we cuddle on my couch and you whisper sweet romantic nothings in my ear."

"I'd prefer to whisper sweet somethings."

She swung into my arms. "You just think you can coerce me into the bedroom with talk like that."

"Hm," I said.

We kissed, taking our time, long and deeply, and kids whistled in the distance. When we broke apart she asked, "Will you be visiting much?"

I thought about phone calls at four in the morning, either from Michelle or Anna, involving guys named Noose or not, and about books I needed to sell and buy and how much of a bonus I should pay Debi when I returned, and whether or not the goulash really did have sentience and was at this moment plotting its gray escape from the fridge, and how Lowell had looked at me, and Broghin and Lisa and Doug, and how good it felt to have a woman I cared about stitch me up when I bled and help keep me from further scarring, and how much better it would be to coerce her into the bedroom.

"Yes," I said.